Frivolous Cupid

Frivolous Cupid

Anthony Hope

WAKING LION PRESS

ISBN 1-60096-143-6

Published by Waking Lion Press, an imprint of The Editorium

Waking Lion Press™, the Waking Lion Press logo, and The Editorium™ are trademarks of The Editorium, LLC

The Editorium, LLC
West Valley City, UT 84128-3917
wakinglionpress.com
wakinglion@editorium.com

Contents

Chapter 1

Reluctance

I.

Neither life nor the lawn-tennis club was so full at Natterley that the news of Harry Sterling's return had not some importance.

He came back, moreover, to assume a position very different from his old one. He had left Harrow now, departing in the sweet aroma of a long score against Eton at Lord's, and was to go up to Oxford in October. Now between a schoolboy and a University man there is a gulf, indicated unmistakably by the cigarette which adorned Harry's mouth as he walked down the street with a newly acquiescent father, and thoroughly realized by his old playmates. The young men greeted him as an equal, the boys grudgingly accepted his superiority, and the girls received him much as though they had never met him before in their lives and were pressingly in need of an introduction. These features of his reappearance amused Mrs. Mortimer; she recollected him as an untidy, shy, pretty boy; but mind, working on matter, had so transformed him that she was doubtful enough about him to ask her husband if that were really Harry Sterling.

Mr. Mortimer, mopping his bald head after one of his energetic failures at lawn tennis, grunted assent, and remarked that a few years more would see a like development in their elder son, a remark which bordered on absurdity; for Johnny was but eight, and ten years are not a few years to a lady of twenty-eight, whatever they may seem to a man of forty-four.

Presently Harry, shaking himself free from an entangling group of the Vicarage girls, joined his father, and the two came across to Mrs. Mortimer.

She was a favorite of old Sterling's, and he was proud to present his handsome son to her. She listened graciously to his jocosities, stealing a glance at Harry when his father called him "a good boy." Harry blushed and assumed an air of indifference, tossing his hair back from his smooth forehead, and swinging his racket carelessly in his hand. The lady addressed some words of patronizing kindness to him, seeking to put him at his ease. She seemed to succeed to some extent, for he let his father and her husband go off together, and sat down by her on the bench, regardless of the fact that the Vicarage girls were waiting for him to make a fourth.

He said nothing, and Mrs. Mortimer looked at him from under her long lashes; in so doing she discovered that he was looking at her.

"Aren't you going to play any more, Mr. Sterling?" she asked.

"Why aren't you playing?" he rejoined.

"My husband says I play too badly."

"Oh, play with me! We shall make a good pair."

"Then you must be very good."

"Well, no one can play a hang here, you know. Besides I'm sure you're all right, really."

"You forget my weight of years."

He opened his blue eyes a little, and laughed. He was, in fact, astonished to find that she was quite a young woman. Remembering old Mortimer and the babies, he had thought of her as full middle-aged. But she was not; nor had she that likeness to a suet pudding, which his newborn critical faculty cruelly detected in his old friends, the Vicarage girls.

There was one of them—Maudie—with whom he had flirted in his holidays; he wondered at that, especially when a relentless memory told him that Mrs. Mortimer must have been at the parties where the thing went on. He felt very much older, so much older that

Mrs. Mortimer became at once a contemporary. Why, then, should she begin, as she now did, to talk to him, in quasi maternal fashion, about his prospects? Men don't have prospects, or, anyhow, are spared questionings thereon.

Either from impatience of this topic, or because, after all, tennis was not to be neglected, he left her, and she sat alone for a little while, watching him play. She was glad that she had not played; she could not have rivaled the activity of the Vicarage girls. She got up and joined Mrs. Sterling, who was presiding over the club teapot. The good lady expected compliments on her son, but for some reason Mrs. Mortimer gave her none. Very soon, indeed, she took Johnnie away with her, leaving her husband to follow at his leisure.

In comparing Maudie Sinclair to a suet pudding, Harry had looked at the dark side of the matter.

The suggestion, though indisputable, was only occasionally obtrusive, and as a rule hushed almost to silence by the pleasant good nature which redeemed shapeless features. Mrs. Mortimer had always liked Maudie, who ran in and out of her house continually, and had made of herself a vice-mother to the little children.

The very next day she came, and, in the intervals of playing cricket with Johnnie, took occasion to inform Mrs. Mortimer that in her opinion Harry Sterling was by no means improved by his new status and dignity. She went so far as to use the term "stuck-up." "He didn't use to be like that," she said, shaking her head; "he used to be very jolly." Mrs. Mortimer was relieved to note an entire absence of romance either in the regretted past or the condemned present. Maudie mourned a friend spoiled, not an admirer lost; the tone of her criticisms left no doubt of it, and Mrs. Mortimer, with a laugh, announced her intention of asking the Sterlings to dinner and having Maudie to meet them. "You will be able to make it up then," said she.

"Why, I see him every day at the tennis club," cried Maudie in surprise.

The faintest of blushes tinged Mrs. Mortimer's cheek as she chid herself for forgetting this obvious fact.

The situation now developed rapidly. The absurd thing happened: Harry Sterling began to take a serious view of his attachment to Mrs. Mortimer. The one thing more absurd, that she should take a serious view of it, had not happened yet, and, indeed, would never happen; so she told herself with a nervous little laugh. Harry gave her no opportunity of saying so to him, for you cannot reprove glances or discourage pressings of your hand in fashion so blunt.

And he was very discreet: he never made her look foolish. In public he treated her with just the degree of attention that gained his mother's fond eulogium, and his father's approving smile; while Mr. Mortimer, who went to London at nine o'clock every morning and did not return till seven, was very seldom bothered by finding the young fellow hanging about the house. Certainly he came pretty frequently between the hours named, but it was, as the children could have witnessed, to play with them. And, through his comings and goings, Mrs. Mortimer moved with pleasure, vexation, self-contempt, and eagerness.

One night she and her husband went to dine with the Sterlings. After dinner Mr. Mortimer accepted his host's invitation to stay for a smoke. He saw no difficulty in his wife walking home alone; it was but half a mile, and the night was fine and moonlit. Mrs. Mortimer made no difficulty either, but Mrs. Sterling was sure that Harry would be delighted to see Mrs. Mortimer to her house.

She liked the boy to learn habits of politeness, she said, and his father eagerly proffered his escort, waving aside Mrs. Mortimer's protest that she would not think of troubling Mr. Harry; throughout which conversation Harry said nothing at all, but stood smiling, with his hat in his hand, the picture of an obedient, well-mannered youth. There are generally two ways anywhere, and there were two from the Sterlings' to the Mortimers': the short one through the village, and the long one round by the lane and across the Church meadow. The path diverging to the latter route comes very soon after you leave the Sterlings,' and not a word had passed when Mrs. Mortimer and Harry reached it. Still without a word, Harry turned off to follow the path. Mrs. Mortimer glanced at him; Harry smiled.

"It's much longer," she said.

"There's lots of time," rejoined Harry, "and it's such a jolly night." The better to enjoy the night's beauty, he slackened his pace to a very crawl.

"It's rather dark; won't you take my arm?" he said.

"What nonsense! Why, I could see to read!"

"But I'm sure you're tired."

"How absurd you are! Was it a great bore?"

"What?"

"Why, coming."

"No," said Harry.

In such affairs monosyllables are danger signals. A long protestation might have meant nothing: in this short, sufficient negative Mrs. Mortimer recognized the boy's sincerity. A little thrill of pride and shame, and perhaps something else, ran through her. The night was hot and she unfastened the clasp of her cloak, breathing a trifle quickly. To relieve the silence, she said, with a laugh:

"You see we poor married women have to depend on charity. Our husbands don't care to walk home with us. Your father was bent on your coming."

Harry laughed a short laugh; the utter darkness of Mr. Sterling's condition struck through his agitation down to his sense of humor. Mrs. Mortimer smiled at him; she could not help it: the secret between them was so pleasant to her, even while she hated herself for its existence.

They had reached the meadow now, halfway through their journey. A little gate led into it and Harry stopped, leaning his arm on the top rail.

"Oh, no! we must go on," she murmured.

"They won't move for an hour yet," he answered, and then he suddenly broke out:

"How—how funny it is! I hardly remembered you, you know."

"Oh, but I remembered you, a pretty little boy;" and she looked up at his face, half a foot above her. Mere stature has much effect and the little boy stage seemed very far away. And he knew that it did, for he put out his hand to take hers. She drew back.

"No," she said.

5

Harry blushed. She took hold of the gate and he, yielding his place, let her pass through. For a minute or two they walked on in silence.

"Oh, how silly you are!" she cried then, beginning with a laugh and ending with a strange catch in her throat. "Why, you're only just out of knickerbockers!"

"I don't care, I don't care, Hilda—"

"Hush, hush! Oh, indeed, you must be quiet! See, we are nearly home."

He seized her hand, not to be quelled this time, and, bending low over it, kissed it. She did not draw it away, but watched him with a curious, pained smile. He looked up in her face, his own glowing with excitement. He righted himself to his full stature and, from that stooping, kissed her on the lips.

"Oh, you silly boy!" she moaned, and found herself alone in the meadow. He had gone swiftly back by the way they had come, and she went on to her home.

"Well, the boy saw you home?" asked Mr. Mortimer when he arrived half an hour later.

"Yes," she said, raising her head from the cushions of the sofa on which he found her lying.

"I supposed so, but he didn't come into the smoking-room when he got back. Went straight to bed, I expect. He's a nice-mannered young fellow, isn't he?"

"Oh, very!" said Mrs. Mortimer.

II.

Mr. Mortimer had never been so looked after, cosseted, and comforted for his early start as the next morning, nor the children found their mother so patient and affectionate. She was in an abasement of shame and disgust at herself, and quite unable to treat her transgression lightly. That he was a boy and she—not a girl—seemed to charge her with his as well as her own sins, and, besides this moral aggravation, entailed a lower anxiety as to his discretion and secrecy that drove her half mad with worry. Suppose he should boast of it! Or, if he were not bad enough for that, only suppose he should be carried away into carelessness about it! He had nothing to fear worse than what he would call "a wigging" and perhaps summary dismissal to a tutor's: she had more at risk than she could bear to think of. Probably, by now, he recognized his foolishness, and laughed at himself and her. This thought made her no happier, for men may do all that—and yet, very often, they do not stop.

She had to go to a party at the Vicarage in the afternoon. Harry would be sure to be there, and, with a conflict of feeling finding expression in her acts, she protected herself by taking all the children, while she inconsistently dressed herself in her most youthful and coquettish costume. She found herself almost grudging Johnnie his rapidly increasing inches, even while she relied on him for an assertion of her position as a matron. For the folly of last night was to be over and done with, and her acquaintance with Harry Sterling to return to its only possible sane basis; that she was resolved on, but she wanted Harry honestly—even keenly—to regret her determination.

He was talking to Maudie Sinclair when she arrived; he took off his hat, but did not allow his eyes to meet hers. She gathered her children round her, and sat down among the chaperons. Mrs. Sterling came and talked to her; divining a sympathy, the good mother had much to say of her son, of her hopes and her fears for him; so many dangers beset young men, especially if they were attractive, like Harry; there were debts, idleness, fast men, and—worst of all—there were designing women, ready to impose on and ruin the innocence of youth.

"He's been such a good boy till now," said Mrs. Sterling, "but, of course, his father and I feel anxious. If we could only keep him here, out of harm's way, under our own eyes!"

Mrs. Mortimer murmured consolation.

"How kind of you! And your influence is so good for him. He thinks such a lot of you, Hilda."

Mrs. Mortimer, tried too hard, rose and strolled away. Harry's set seemed to end almost directly, and a moment later he was shaking hands with her, still keeping his eyes away from hers. She made her grasp cold and inanimate, and he divined the displeasure she meant to indicate.

"You must go and play again," she said, "or talk to the girls. You mustn't come and talk to me."

"Why not! How can I help it—now?"

The laughing at her and himself had evidently not come, but, bad as that would have been to bear, his tone threatened something worse.

"Don't," she answered sharply. "I'm very angry. You were very unkind and—and ungentlemanly last night."

He flushed crimson.

"Didn't you like it?" he asked, with the terrible simplicity of his youth.

For all her trouble, she had to bite her lip to hide a smile. What a question to ask—just in so many words!

"It was very, very wicked, and, of course, I didn't like it," she answered. "Oh, Harry! don't you know how wicked it was?"

"Oh, yes! I know that, of course," said he, picking at the straw of his hat, which he was carrying in his hand.

"Well, then!" she said.

"I couldn't help it."

"You must help it. Oh, don't you know—oh, it's absurd! I'm years older than you."

"You looked so—so awfully pretty."

"I can't stand talking to you. They'll all see."

"Oh, it's all right. You're a friend of mother's, you know. I say, when shall I be able to see you again—alone, you know?"

Mrs. Mortimer was within an ace of a burst of tears. He seemed not to know that he made her faint with shame, and mad with exultation, and bewildered with terror all in a moment. His new manhood took no heed, save of itself. Was this being out of harm's way, under the eyes of those poor blind parents?

"If—if you care the least for me—for what I wish, go away, Harry," she whispered.

He looked at her in wonder, but, with a frown on his face, did as he was told. Five minutes later he was playing again; she heard him shout "Thirty—love," as he served, a note of triumphant battle in his voice. She believed that she was altogether out of his thoughts.

Her husband was to dine in town that night, and, for sheer protection, she made Maudie Sinclair come and share her evening meal. The children were put to bed, and they sat down alone together, talking over the party. Maudie was pleased to relax a little of her severity toward Harry Sterling; she admitted that he had been very useful in arranging the sets, and very pleasant to everyone.

"Of course, he's conceited," she said, "but all boys are. He'll get over it."

"You talk as if you were a hundred, Maudie," laughed Mrs. Mortimer. "He's older than you are."

"Oh, but boys are much younger than girls, Mrs. Mortimer. Harry Sterling's quite a boy still."

A knock sounded at the door. A minute later the boy walked in. The sight of Maudie Sinclair produced a momentary start, but he recovered himself and delivered a note from his mother, the excuse for his visit. It was an invitation for a few days ahead; there could certainly have been no hurry for it to arrive that night. While Mrs. Mortimer read it, Harry sat down and looked at her. She was obliged to treat his arrival as unimportant, and invited him to have a glass of wine.

"Why are you in evening dress?" asked Maudie wonderingly.

"For dinner," answered Harry.

"Do you dress when you're alone at home?"

"Generally. Most men do."

Maudie allowed herself to laugh. Mrs. Mortimer saw the joke, too, but its amusement was bitter to her.

"I like it," she said gently. "Most of the men I know do it."

"Your husband doesn't," observed Miss Sinclair.

"Poor George gets down from town so tired."

She gave Harry the reply she had written (it was a refusal—she could not have told why), but he seemed not to understand that he was to go. Before he apprehended, she had to give him a significant glance; she gave it in dread of Maudie's eyes. She knew how sharp schoolgirls' eyes are in such things. Whether Maudie saw it or not, Harry did; he sprang to his feet and said good-night.

Maudie was not long after him. The conversation languished, and there was nothing to keep her. With an honest yawn she took her leave. Mrs. Mortimer accompanied her down the garden to the gate. As she went, she became to her startled horror aware of a third person in the garden. She got rid of Maudie as soon as she could, and turned back to the house. Harry, emerging from behind a tree, stood before her.

"I know what you're going to say," he said doggedly, "but I couldn't help it. I was dying to see you again." She spread out her hands as though to push him away. She was like a frightened girl.

"Oh, you're mad!" she whispered. "You must go. Suppose anyone should come. Suppose my husband—"

"I can't help it. I won't stay long."

"Harry, Harry, don't be cruel! You'll ruin me, Harry. If you love me, go—if you love me."

Even now he hardly fathomed her distress, but she had made him understand that this spot and this time were too dangerous.

"Tell me where I can see you safely," he asked, almost demanded.

"You can see me safely—nowhere."

"Nowhere? You mean that you won't—"

"Harry, come here a minute—there—no closer. I just want to be able to touch your hair. Go away, dear—yes, I said 'dear.' Do please go away. You—you won't be any happier afterward for having—if— if you don't go away."

He stood irresolutely still. Her fingers lightly touched his hair, and then her arm dropped at her side. He saw a tear run down her cheek. Suddenly his own face turned crimson.

"I'm—I'm very sorry," he muttered. "I didn't mean—"

"Good-night. I'm going in."

She held out her hand. Again he bent and kissed it, and, as he did so, he felt the light touch of her lips among his hair.

"I'm such a foolish, foolish woman," she whispered, "but you're a gentleman, Harry," and she drew her hand away and left him.

Two days later she took her children off to the seaside. And the Mortimers never came back to Natterley. She wrote and told Mrs. Sterling that George wanted to be nearer his work in town, and that they had gone to live at Wimbledon.

"How we shall miss her!" exclaimed good Mrs. Sterling. "Poor Harry! what'll he say?"

III.

One day, at Brighton, some six years later, a lady in widow's weeds, accompanied by a long, loose-limbed boy of fourteen, was taking the air by the sea. The place was full of people, and the scene gay.

Mrs. Mortimer sat down on a seat and Johnnie stood idly by her. Presently a young man and a girl came along. While they were still a long way off, Mrs. Mortimer, who was looking in that direction, suddenly leaned forward, started a little, and looked hard at them. Johnnie, noticing nothing, whistled unconcernedly.

The couple drew near. Mrs. Mortimer sat with a faint smile on her face. The girl was chatting merrily to the young man, and he listened to her and laughed every now and then, but his bright eyes were not fixed on her, but were here, there, and everywhere, where metal attractive to such eyes might be found. The discursive mood of the eyes somehow pleased Mrs. Mortimer. Just as the young man came opposite her, he glanced in her direction.

Mrs. Mortimer wore the curious, half-indifferent, half-expectant air of one ready for recognition, but not claiming it as a right.

At the first glance, a puzzled look came into the young man's eyes. He looked again: then there was a blank in his eyes. Mrs. Mortimer made no sign, but sat still, half-expectant. He was past her now, but he flung a last glance over his shoulder. He was evidently very doubtful whether the lady on the seat, in the heavy mourning robes, were someone he knew or not. First he thought she was, and then he thought she wasn't. The face certainly reminded him of—now who the deuce was it? Harry knit his brows and exclaimed:

"I half believe that's somebody I know!"

Reluctance

And he puzzled over it, for nearly five minutes, all in vain. Meanwhile Mrs. Mortimer looked at the sea, till Johnnie told her that it was dinner-time.

Chapter 2

Why Men Don't Marry

We were sitting around the fire at Colonel Holborow's. Dinner was over—had, in fact, been over for some time—the hour of smoke, whisky, and confidence had arrived, and we had been telling one another the various reasons which accounted for our being unmarried, for we were all bachelors except the colonel, and he had, as a variety, told the reasons why he wished he was unmarried (his wife was away). Jack Dexter, however, had not spoken, and it was only in response to a direct appeal that he related the following story. The story may be true or untrue, but I must remark that Jack always had rather a weakness for representing himself on terms of condescending intimacy with the nobility and even greater folk.

Jack sighed deeply. There was a sympathetic silence. Then he began:

"For some reason best known to herself," said Jack, with a patient shrug of his shoulders, "the Duchess of Medmenham (I don't know whether any of you fellows know her) chose to object to me as a suitor for the hand of her daughter, Mary Fitzmoine. The woman was so ignorant that she may really have thought that my birth was not equal to her daughter's; but all the world knows that the Munns were yeomen two hundred years ago, and that her Grace's family hails from a stucco villa in the neighborhood of Cardiff. However, the duchess did object; and when the season (in the course of which I had met Lady Mary many times) ended, instead of allowing her daughter to pay a series of visits at houses where I had arranged to be, she sent her off to Switzerland, under the care of a dragon whom she had engaged to keep me and other dangerous fellows at a proper distance. On hearing of what had happened from George Fitzmoine (an intimate friend of mine), I at once threw up my visits and started in pursuit. I felt confident that Lady Mary was favorably inclined (in fact, I had certain proofs which—but no matter), and that if I won her heart I could break down the old lady's opposition. I should certainly have succeeded in my enterprise, and been at this moment the husband of one of the most beautiful girls in England, but for a very curious and unfortunate circumstance, which placed me in an unfavorable light in Mary's eyes. I was not to blame; it was just a bit of bad luck.

"I ranged over most of Switzerland in search of Lady Mary. Wherever I went I asked about her, and at last I got upon the track. At Interlaken I found her name in the visitors' book, together with that of a Miss Dibbs, whom I took to be the dragon.

I questioned the porter and found that the two ladies had, the afternoon before, hired a carriage and driven to a quiet little village some fifteen miles off, where there was a small but good inn. Here they evidently meant to stay, for letters were to be sent after them there for the next week. The place was described to me as pretty and retired; it seemed, therefore, an ideal spot for my purpose. I made up my mind at once. I started the next day after luncheon, took the journey easily, and came in sight of the little inn about seven o'clock in the evening. All went well. The only question was as to the disposition of Miss Dibbs toward me. I prayed that she might turn out to be a romantic dragon; but, in case she should prove obstinate, I made my approaches with all possible caution. When my carriage stopped at the door I jumped out. The head waiter, a big fellow in a white waistcoat, was on the steps. I drew him aside, and took a ten-franc piece from my pocket.

"'Is there a young lady staying here?' I asked. 'Tall, fair, handsome?' and I slid the piece of gold into his palm.

"'Well, yes, sir,' he said, 'there is a young lady, and she is all that you say, sir. Pardon me, Monsieur is English?'

"'Yes,' said I.

"'Ah,' said he, smiling mysteriously. 'And it is Wednesday.'

"'It is certainly Wednesday,' I admitted, though I did not see that the day of the week mattered much.

"He came close to me and whispered:

"'The lady thought you might come, sir. I think she expects you, sir. Oh, you can rely on my discretion, sir.'

"I was rather surprised, but not very much, for I had hinted to George Fitzmoine that I meant to try my luck, and I supposed that he had passed my hint on to his sister. My predominant feeling was one of gratification. Mary loved me! Mary expected me! There was complete mental sympathy between Mary and myself!

"I went up to my room in a state of great contentment. I had been there about half an hour when my friend the waiter came in. Advancing toward me with a mysterious air, he took a blank envelope out of his pocket and held it up before me with a roguish smile.

"'Monsieur will know the handwriting inside,' he said cunningly.

"Now I had never corresponded with Lady Mary, and of course did not know her handwriting, but I saw no use in telling the waiter that. In truth, I thought the fellow quite familiar enough. So I said shortly and with some hauteur:

"'Give me the note;' and I took another piece of gold out of my pocket. We exchanged our possessions, the waiter withdrew with a wink, and I tore open the precious note.

"'Whatever you do,' it ran, 'don't recognize me. I am *watched*. As soon as I can I will tell you where to meet me. I knew you would come.—M.'

"'The darling!' I exclaimed. 'She's a girl of spirit. I'll take good care not to betray her. Oh, we'll circumvent old Dibbs between us.'

"At eight o'clock I went down to the salle a manger. It was quite empty. Mary and Miss Dibbs no doubt dined in their own sitting room, and there appeared to be no one else in the hotel. However, when I was halfway through my meal, a stylishly dressed young woman came in and sat down at a table at the end of the room farthest from where I was. I should have noticed her more, but I was in a reverie about Mary's admirable charms, and I only just looked at her; she was frowning and drumming angrily with her fingers on the table. The head waiter hurried up to her; his face was covered with smiles, and he gave me a confidential nod en passant. Nothing else occurred except that a villainous looking fellow—something, to judge by his appearance, between a valet and a secretary—thrust his ugly head through the door three or four times. Whenever he did so the waiter smiled blandly at him. He did it the last time just as the lady was walking down the room. Seeing her coming he drew back and held the door open for her with a clumsy, apologetic bow. She smiled scornfully and passed through. The waiter stood grinning in the middle of the room, and when I, in my turn, rose, he whispered to me, 'It's all right, sir.' I went to bed and dreamed of Mary.

"On entering the room next morning the first person I saw was Mary. She was looking adorably fresh and pretty. She sat opposite a stout, severe-looking dame in black. Directly my eyes alighted on her I schooled them into a studiously vacant expression. She, poor girl, was no diplomatist. She started; she glanced anxiously at Miss Dibbs; I saw her lips move; she blushed; she seemed almost to smile. Of course this behavior (I loved Mary the more that she could not conceal her delightful embarrassment!) excited the dragon's curiosity; she turned round and favored me with a searching gaze. I was equal to the occasion. I comprehended them both in a long, cool, deliberate, empty stare. The strain on my self-control was immense, but I supported it. Mary blushed crimson, and her eyes sank to her plate. Poor girl! She had sadly overrated her powers of deception. I was not surprised that Miss Dibbs frowned severely and sniffed audibly.

"At that moment the other girl came in. She walked up, took the table next to mine, and, to my confusion, bestowed upon me a look of evident interest, though of the utmost shortness—one of those looks, you know, that seem to be repented of in an instant, and are generally the most deliberate. I took no notice at all, assuming an air of entire unconsciousness. A few minutes later Mary got up and made for the door, with Miss Dibbs in close attendance. The imprudent child could not forbear to glance at me; but I, seeing the dragon's watchful eye upon me, remained absolutely irresponsive.

Nay, to throw Miss Dibbs off the scent, I fixed my eyes on my neighbor with assumed preoccupation. Flushing painfully, Mary hurried out, and I heard Miss Dibbs sniff again. I chuckled over her obvious disapproval of my neighbor and myself. The excellent woman evidently thought us no better than we ought to be! But I felt that I should go mad if I could not speak to Mary soon.

"I went out and sat down in the veranda. It was then about half-past ten. The ugly fellow whom I had noticed the evening before was hanging about, but presently a waiter came and spoke to him, and he got up with a grumble and went into the house. Ten minutes afterward my neighbor of the salle a manger came out. She looked very discontented. She rang a handbell that stood on the table, and a waiter ran up.

"'Where's the head waiter?' she asked sharply.

"'Pardon, ma'mselle, but he is waiting on some ladies upstairs.'

"'What a nuisance!' said she. 'But you'll do. I want to give him an order. Stay; come indoors and I'll write it down.'

"She disappeared, and I sat on, wondering how I was to get a sight of Mary. At last, in weariness, I went indoors to the smoking room. It looked out to the back and was a dreary little room; but I lit my cigar and began on a three days' old copy of the Times. Thus I spent a tedious hour. Then my friend the head waiter appeared, looking more roguish than ever. I dived into my pocket, he produced a note, I seized it.

"'Why have you been so long?' (Charmingly unreasonable! what could I have done?) 'Directly you get this, come to the wood behind the hotel. Take the path to the right and go straight till you find me. I have thrown the *spy* [poor old Dibbs!] off the scent.—M.'

"I caught up my hat and rushed into the hall. I cannoned into a young man who had just got out of a carriage and was standing in the veranda. With a hasty apology I dashed on. Beyond doubt she loved me! And she was honest enough not to conceal it. I hate mock modesty. I longed to show her how truly I returned her love, and I rejoiced that there need be no tedious preliminaries.

Mary and I understood one another. A kiss would be the seal of our love—and the most suitable beginning of our conversation.

"In five minutes I was in the wood. Just before I disappeared among its trees I heard someone calling 'Monsieur, monsieur!' It sounded like the voice of the head waiter, but I wouldn't have stopped for fifty head waiters. I took the path Mary had indicated and ran along it at the top of my speed. Suddenly, to my joy, I caught sight of the figure of a girl; she was seated on a mound of grass, and, though her face was from me, I made no doubt it was Mary. She wore the most charming blue cloak (it was a chilly morning) which completely enveloped her. I determined not to shilly-shally. She loved me—I loved her. I ran forward, plumped down on my knees behind her, took her head between my hands dodged round, and kissed her cheek.

"'At last, my darling!' I cried in passionate tones.

"By Jupiter, it was the other girl, though!

"I sprang back in horror. The girl looked at me for a moment. Then she blushed; then she frowned; then—why, then she began to laugh consumedly. I was amazed.

"'"At last," you call it,' she gasped. 'I call it "at first"'; and she laughed merrily and melodiously. She certainly had a nice laugh, that girl.

"Now, concerning what follows, I have, since then, entertained some doubts whether I behaved in all respects discreetly. You will allow that the position was a difficult one, but it is, I admit, very possible that my wisest course would have been to make an apology and turn tail as quickly as I could. Well, I didn't. I thought that I owed the lady a full explanation. Besides, I wanted a full explanation myself. Finally (oh, yes, I see you fellows grinning and winking), Mary was not there, and this young lady rather interested me. I decided that I would have five minutes' talk with her; then I would run back and find Mary.

"'I must beg a thousand pardons,' I began, 'but I took you for somebody else."

"'Oh, of course,' said she, with a shrug, 'it's always that.'

"'You appear incredulous,' said I, rather offended.

"'Well, and if I am?' said she.

"My feelings were hurt. I produced Mary's second note.

18

"'If I can trust to your discretion, I'll prove what I say,' I remarked in a nettled tone.

"'I shall be very curious to hear the proof, sir, and I will be most discreet,' she said. She was pouting, but her eyes danced. Really, she looked very pretty—although, of course, I would not for a moment compare her with Lady Mary.

"'A lady,' said I, 'was so kind as to tell me to seek her here this morning.'

"'Oh, as if I believed that!'

"I was piqued.

"'There's the proof,' I cried, flinging the note into her lap.

"She took it up, glanced at it, and gave a little shriek.

"'Where did you get this?'

"'Why, from the head waiter.'

"'Oh, the fool!' she cried. 'It's mine.'

"'Yours? nonsense! He gave me that and another last night.'

"'Oh, the stupidity! They were for—they were not for you. They were for—someone who is to arrive.'

"I pointed at the signature and gasped, 'M.! Do you sign M.?'

"'Yes; my name's—my name begins with M. Oh, if I'd only seen that waiter this morning! Oh, the idiot!'

"Then I believe I swore.

"'Madame,' said I, 'I'm ruined! No harm is done to you—I'm a man of honor—but I'm ruined. On the strength of your wretched notes, madame, I've cut the girl I love best in the world—cut her dead—dead—dead!'

"'What? That young lady in the—Oh, you thought they were from her? Oh, I see? How—how—oh, how very amusing!' And the heartless little wretch went off into another peal of laughter.

"'You pretended not to know her! Oh, dear! oh, dear!' and her laughter echoed among the trees again. 'I saw her looking at you, and you ate on like a pig! Oh, dear! oh, dear!'

"'Stop laughing!' said I savagely.

"'Oh, I'm very sorry, but I can't. What a scrape you've go into! Oh, me!' And she wiped her eyes (they were as blue as her cloak) with a delicate bit of a handkerchief.

"'You shan't laugh,' said I. 'Who were your notes for?'

"'Somebody I expected. He hasn't come. The waiter took you for him, I suppose. I never thought of his being so stupid. Oh, what a brute she must have thought you!' And she began to laugh again.

"I had had enough of it. I hate being laughed at.

"'If you go on laughing,' said I, 'I'll kiss you again.'

"The threat was a failure; she did not appear at all alarmed.

"'Not you!' she said, laughing worse than ever.

"I should like you fellows to understand that my heart never wavered in its allegiance to Lady Mary—my conscience is quite clear as to that—but I had pledged my word. I caught that tiresome girl round the waist and I kissed her once—I'm sure of once, anyhow. She gasped and struggled, laughing still. Then, with a sudden change of voice, she cried, 'Stop,' stop!'

"I let her go. I looked round. We had a gallery of spectators. On one side stood the ugly-headed valet; on the other, in attitudes of horror, Mary and Miss Dibbs!

"'You've ruined us both now,' said the girl in blue.

"I rose to my feet and was about to explain, when the ugly fellow rushed at me, brandishing a cane. I had quite enough to arrange without being bothered by him. I caught the cane in my left hand, and with my right I knocked him down.

"Then I walked up to Lady Mary. I took no heed of Miss Dibbs' presence; it was too critical a moment to think of trifles.

"'Lady Mary,' said I, 'appearances are so much against me that you cannot possibly attach the slightest weight to them.'

"'Sir,' said she, 'I have no longer the honor of your acquaintance. I have only to thank you for having had the consideration not to recognize me when we met so unexpectedly in the dining room. Pray continue to show me the same favor.'

"With which pleasant little speech she turned on her heel. It was clear that she suspected me most unjustly. I turned to the girl in blue, but she was beforehand with me.

"Ah, I wish I'd never see you,' she cried, 'you great, stupid creature! He [she pointed to the prostrate figure of the ugly servant] will tell Frederic everything.'

"'Come,' said I, '_I_ was only an accident; it would have been just as bad if—'

"As I spoke I heard a step behind me. Turning round, I found myself face to face with the young man with whom I had come in collision as I rushed through the hall. He gazed at the servant—at me—at the girl in blue.

"'Margaret!' he exclaimed, 'what is the—'

"'Hush, hush!' she whispered, pointing again to the servant.

"I stepped up to him, lifting my hat:

"'Sir,' said I, "kindly inform me if you are the gentleman who was to come from England.'

"'Certainly I come from England,' he said.

"'And you ought to have arrived on Wednesday?'

"'Yes," he answered.

"'Then,' said I, 'all I have to say to you, sir, is—that I wish to the devil you'd keep your appointments.' And I left them.

"That's why I'm not married, boys. Where's my glass?"

"It is a very curious story," observed the colonel. "And who were they all—the girl in blue—and the young man—and the ugly servant—and Frederic?"

"Colonel," said Jack, with an air of deepest mystery, "you would be astounded to hear."

We all pricked up our ears.

"But," he continued, "I am not at liberty to say."

We sank back in our chairs.

"Do you know?" asked the colonel, and Jack nodded solemnly.

"Out with it!" we cried.

"Impossible!" said Jack. "But I may tell you that the matter engaged the attention of more than one of the Foreign Offices of Europe."

"Good Heavens!" cried we in chorus, and Jack drank off his whisky and water, rose to his feet, and put on his hat.

"Poor dear Mary!" said he, as he opened the door. "She never got over it."

The colonel shouted after him:

"Then what did she marry Jenkyns of the Blues for?"

"Pique!" said Jack, and he shut the door.

Chapter 3

A Change of Heart

It was common knowledge that Smugg was engaged to be married.

Familiarity had robbed the fact of some of its surprisingness, but there remained a substratum of wonder, not removed even by the sight of his betrothed's photograph and the information that she was a distant relative who had been brought up with him from infancy. The features and the explanation between them rescued Smugg from the incongruity of a romance, but we united in the opinion that the lady was ill-advised in preferring Smugg to solitude. Still, for all that he was a ridiculous creature, she did, and hence it happened that Smugg, desiring to form a furnishing fund, organized a reading party, which Gayford, Tritton, Bird, and I at once joined.

Every morning at nine Smugg, his breakfast finished, cleared his corner of the table, opened his books, and assumed an expectant air; so Mary the maid told us; we were never there ourselves; we breakfasted at 9.30 or 10 o'clock, and only about 11 did we clear our corners, light our pipes, open our books, and discuss the prospects of the day.

As we discussed them, Smugg construed in a gentle bleat; what he construed or why he construed it (seeing that nobody heeded him) was a mystery; the whole performance was simply a tribute to Smugg's conscience, and, as such, was received with good-natured, scornful toleration.

Suddenly a change came.

One morning there was no Smugg! Yet he had breakfasted—Mary and an eggshell testified to that effect. He reappeared at 11.30, confused and very warm (he had exceptional powers in the way of being warm). We said nothing, and he began to bleat Horace. In a minute of silence I happened to hear what it was: it referred to a lady of the name of Pyrrha; the learned may identify the passage for themselves. The next day the same thing happened except that it was close on twelve before Smugg appeared. Gayford and Tritton took no notice of the aberration; Bird congratulated Smugg on the increased docility of his conscience. I watched him closely as he wiped his brow— he was very warm, indeed. A third time the scene was enacted; my curiosity was aroused; I made Mary call me very early, and from the window I espied Smugg leaving the house at 9.15, and going with rapid, furtive steps along the little path that led to old Dill's tiny farm. I slipped downstairs, bolted a cup of tea, seized a piece of toast, and followed Smugg. He was out of sight, but presently I met Joe Shanks, the butcher's son, who brought us our chops. Joe was a stout young man, about twenty-one, red-faced, burly, and greasy. We used to have many jokes with Joe; even Smugg had before now broken a mild shaft of classical wit on him; in fact, we made a butt of Joe, and his good-humored, muttony smile told us that he thought it a compliment.

"Seen Mr. Smugg as you came along, Joe?" I asked.

"Yes, sir. Gone toward Dill's farm, sir."

"Ah, Dill's farm!"

"Yes, sir."

The chop-laden Joe passed on. I mended my pace, and soon found myself on the outskirts of Dill's premises. I had been there before; we had all been there before. Dill had a daughter. I saw her now in a sunbonnet and laced boots. I may say at once that Betsy Dill was very pretty, in a fine, robust style, and all four of us were decidedly enamored of her charms. Usually we courted her in a body, and scrupulous fairness was observed in the matter of seeking private interviews.

Smugg had never spoken to her—so we should all have sworn. But now my wondering eyes saw, opposite Pyrrha (we began from this day to call her Pyrrha) the figure of Smugg. Pyrrha was leaning against a barn, one foot crossed over the other, her arms akimbo, a string of her bonnet in her mouth, and her blue eyes laughing from under long lashes. Smugg stood limply opposite her, his trousers bagging over his half-bent knees, his hat in one hand, and in the other a handkerchief, with which, from time to time, he mopped his forehead. I could not hear (of course I did not wish to) what they were saying; indeed, I have my doubts if they said anything; but presently Smugg moved a hesitating step nearer, when Pyrrha, with a merry laugh, darted by him and ran away, turning a mocking face over her shoulder. Smugg stood still for a minute, then put on his hat, looked at his watch, and walked slowly away.

I did not keep Smugg's secret; I felt under no obligation to keep it. He deserved no mercy, and I exposed him at breakfast that very morning. But I could not help being a little sorry for him when he came in. He bent his head under the shower of reproach, chaff, and gibing; he did not try to excuse himself; he simply opened his book at the old place, and we all shouted the old ode, substituting "Betsa" for "Pyrrha" wherever we could. Still, in spite of our jocularity, we all felt an under-current of real anger.

We considered that Smugg was treating Pyrrha very badly—Smugg, an engaged man, aged thirty, presumably past the heat and carelessness of youth. We glowed with a sense of her wrongs, and that afternoon we each went for a solitary walk—at least, we started for a solitary walk—but half an hour later we all met at the gate leading to Dill's meadows, and, in an explosion of laughter, acknowledged our secret design of meeting Pyrrha, and opening her eyes to Smugg's iniquity.

The great surprise was still to come. At eleven the next morning, when we had just sat down to work, and Smugg had slid into the room with the stealthy, ashamed air he wore after his morning excursions, Mary appeared, and told us that Joe Shanks, the butcher's son, had come with the chops, and wanted to speak to us. We hailed the diversion, and had Joe shown in. Gayford pushed the beer jug and a glass toward him, saying:

"Help yourself, Joe."

Joe drank a draught, wiped his mouth on his blue sleeve, and remarked:

"No offense, gentlemen."

"None," said Gayford, who seemed to have assumed the chairmanship of the meeting.

Joe, seeming slightly embarrassed, cleared his throat, and looked round again.

"No offense, gentlemen," he repeated; "but she's bin walking with me two years come Michaelmas."

A pause followed. Then the chairman expressed the views of the meeting.

"The deuce she has!" said he.

"Off *and* on," added Joe candidly.

I looked at Smugg. He had shrunk down low in his seat, and rested his head on his hand. His face was half hidden; but he was very warm, and the drops trickled from his forehead down his nose.

"It seems to be a good deal off," said the chairman judicially.

"No offense," said Joe; "but I don't take it kind of you, gentlemen. I've served you faithful."

"The chops are excellent," conceded the chairman.

"And I don't take it kind."

"Develop your complaint," said the chairman. "I mean, what's the row, Joe?"

"Since you gentlemen came she's been saucy," said Joe.

"I do not see," observed the chairman, "that anything can be done. If Pyrrha prefers us, Joe [he treated the case collectively, which was certainly wise], what then?"

"Beg pardon, sir?"

"Oh, I mean if the lady prefers us, Joe?"

Joe brought his fat fist down on the table with a thump.

"It aint as if you meant it," said he doggedly; "you just unsettles of 'er. I s'pose I can't help ye talking, and laughing, and walking along of 'er, but you aint no call to kiss 'er."

Another pause ensued. The chairman held a consultation with Tritton, who sat on his right hand.

"The meeting," said Gayford, "will proceed to declare, one by one, whether it has ever—and if so, how often—kissed the lady. I will begin. Never! Mr. Tritton?"

"Never!" said Tritton.

"Mr. Bird?"

"Never!" said Bird.

"Mr. Robertson?"

"Never!" said I.

"Mr. Smugg?"

"I seed 'im this very morning!" cried Joe, like an accusing angel.

Smugg took his hand away from his face, after giving his wet brow one last dab. He looked at Gayford and at Joe, but said nothing.

"Mr. Smugg?" repeated the chairman.

"Mr. Smugg," interposed Tritton suavely, "probably feels himself in a difficulty. The secret is not, perhaps, entirely his own."

We all nodded.

"We enter a plea of not guilty for Mr. Smugg," observed the chairman gravely.

"I seed 'im do it," said Joe.

No one spoke. Joe finished his beer, pulled his forelock, and turned on his heel. Suddenly Smugg burst into speech. He could hardly form his words, and they jostled one another in the breathless confusion of his utterance.

"I—I—you've no right. I say nothing. If I choose, I shall—no one has a right to stop me. If I love her—if she doesn't mind—I say nothing—nothing at all. I won't hear a word. I shall do as I like."

Joe had paused to hear him, and now stood looking at him in wonder. Then he stepped quickly up to the table, and, leaning across, asked in a harsh voice:

"You mean honest, do you, by her? You'd make her your wife, would you?"

Smugg, looking straight in front of him, answered:

"Yes."

Joe drew back, touched his forelock again, and said:

"Then it's fair fighting, sir, begging your pardon; and no offense. But the girl was mine first, sir."

27

Then Gayford interposed.

"Mr. Smugg," said he, "you tell Joe, here, that you'd marry this lady. May I ask how you can—when—"

But for once Smugg was able to silence one of his pupils. He arose from his seat, and brought his hand heavily down on Gayford's shoulder.

"Hold your tongue!" he cried. "I must answer to God, but I needn't answer to you."

Joe looked at him with round eyes, and, with a last salute, slowly went out. None of us spoke, and presently Smugg opened his Thucydides.

For my part, I took very considerable interest in Pyrrha's side of the question. I amused myself by constructing a fancy-born love of Pyrrha's for her social superior, and if he had been one of ourselves, I should have seen no absurdity. But Smugg refused altogether to fit into my frame. There was no glamour about Smugg; and, to tell the truth, I should have thought that any girl, be her station what it might, faced with the alternative of Smugg and Joe, would have chosen Joe. In my opinion, Pyrrha was merely amusing herself with Smugg, and I was rather comforted by this reversal of the ordinary roles. Still, I could not rest in conjecture, and my curiosity led me up to Dill's little farm on the afternoon of the day of Joe's sudden appearance. The others let me go alone. Directly after dinner Smugg went to his bedroom, and the other three had gone off to play lawn tennis at the vicar's. I lit my pipe, and strolled along till I reached the gate that led to Dill's meadow. Here I waited till Pyrrha should appear.

As I sat and smoked, a voice struck suddenly on my ear—the voice of Mrs. Dill, raised to shrillness by anger.

"Be off with you," she said, "and mind your ways, or worse '11 happen to you. 'Ere's your switch."

After a moment Pyrrha turned the corner, and came toward me. She was wiping her eyes with the corner of her apron, and carried in her hand a light hazel switch, which she used to guide errant cows. She was almost at the gate before she saw me. She started, and blushed very red.

"Lor! is it you, Mr. Robertson?" she said.

I nodded, but did not move.

"Let me pass, sir, please. I've no time to stop."

"What, not to talk to me, Pyrrha—Betsy, I mean?"

"Mother don't like me talking to gentlemen."

"You've been crying," said I.

"No, I haven't," said Pyrrha, quite violently.

"Mother been scolding you?"

"I wish you'd let me by, sir."

"What for?"

"It's all your fault," burst out Pyrrha. "I didn't want you; no, nor him, either. What do you come and get me into trouble for?"

"I haven't done anything, Betsy. Come now!"

"You aint as bad as some," she conceded, a dim smile breaking through the clouds.

"You mean Smugg," I observed.

"Who told you?" she cried.

"Joe," said I.

"Seems he's got a lot to say to everybody," she commented resentfully.

"Ah! he told your mother, did he? Well, you know you shouldn't, Betsy."

"I won't never speak to him again—I meant I won't ever [the grammarian is abroad], Mr. Robertson."

"What! Not to Joe?"

"Joe! No; that Smugg."

"But Joe told of you."

"Well, and it was his right."

If she thought so, I had no more to say. Notions differ among different sets. But I pressed the point a little.

"Joe got you your scolding."

Now, I can't say whether I did or did not emphasize the last word unduly, but Pyrrha blushed again, and remarked:

"You want to know too much, sir, by a deal."

So I left that aspect to the subject, and continued:

"I suppose it was for letting Mr. Smugg kiss you?"

"I couldn't help it."

I had great doubts of that—she could have tackled Smugg with one hand; but I said pleasantly:

"No more could he, I'm sure."

Pyrrha cast an alarmed glance at the house.

"Oh, I'll be careful," I laughed. "Yes, and I'll let you go. But just tell me, Betsy, what do you think of Mr. Smugg?"

"I don't think that of him!" said she, snapping her pretty red fingers. "Joe 'ud make ten of him. I wish Joe'd talk to him a bit."

The end came soon after this, and, in spite of our attitude (I speak of us four, not of Smugg) of whole-heartedness, I think it was rather a shock to us all, when Joe announced one morning, on his arrival with the chops, that he was to be made a happy man at the church next day. Smugg was not in the room, and the rest of us congratulated Joe, and made up a purse for him to give Pyrrha, with our best respects, and he bowed himself out, mightily pleased, and asseverating that we were real gentlemen. Then we sat and looked at the table.

"It robs us of a resource," pronounced Gayford, once again making himself the mouthpiece of the party. We all nodded, and filled fresh pipes.

Presently Smugg sidled in. We had seen little of him the last week; save when he was construing he had taken refuge in his own room. When he came in now, Gayford wagged his head significantly at me; apparently, it was my task to bell the cat. I rose, and went to the mantelpiece. Smugg had sat down at the table, and my back was to him. I took a match from the box, struck it, and applied it to my pipe, and, punctuating my words with interspersed puffings, I said carelessly:

"By the way, Smugg, Pyrrha's going to be married to Joe Shanks to-morrow."

I don't know how he looked. I kept my face from him, but, after a long minute's pause, he answered:

"Thank you, Robertson. It's Aeschylus this morning, isn't it?"

We had a noisy evening that night. I suppose we felt below par, and wanted cheering up. Anyhow, we made an expedition to the grocer's, and amazed him with a demand for his best champagne and his choicest sherry. We carried the goods home in a bag, and sat down to a revel. Smugg had some bread and cheese in his own room; he said that he had letters to write. We dined largely, and drank still more largely; then we sang, and at last—it was near on twelve, a terrible hour for that neighborhood—we made our way, amid much boisterousness and horseplay, to bed; where I, at least, was asleep in five minutes.

As the church clock struck two, I awoke. I heard a sound of movement in Smugg's room next door. I lay and listened. Presently his door opened, and he creaked gently downstairs. I sprang out of bed and looked out of the window. Smugg, fully dressed, was gliding along the path toward Dill's farm. Some impulse—curiosity only, very likely—made me jump into my trousers, seize a flannel jacket, draw on a pair of boots, and hastily follow him. When I got outside he was visible in the moonlight, mounting the path ahead of me. He held on his way toward the farm, I following. When he reached the yard he stopped for a moment, and seemed to peer up at the windows, which were all dark and unresponsive. I stood as quiet as I could, twenty yards from him, and moved cautiously on again when he turned to the right and passed through the gate into the meadows.

I saw no signs of Pyrrha. Smugg held on his way across the meadows, down toward the stream; and suddenly the thought leaped to my brain that the poor fool meant to drown himself. But I could hardly believe it. Surely he must merely be taking a desperate lover's ramble, a last sad visit to the scenes of his silly, irrational infatuation. If I went up to him, I should look a fool, too; so I hung behind, ready to turn upon him if need appeared.

He walked down to the very edge of the stream; it ran deep and fast just here, under a high bank and a row of old willows. Smugg sat down on the bank, wet though the grass was, and clasped his hands over his knees. I crouched down a little way behind him, ready and alert. I am a good swimmer, and I did not doubt my power to pull him out, even if I were not in time to prevent him jumping in. I saw him rise, look over the brink, and sit down again. I almost thought I saw him shiver. And presently, through the stillness of the summer night, came the strangest, saddest sound; catching my ear as it drifted across the meadow. Smugg was sobbing, and his sobs—never loud—rose and fell with the subdued stress of intolerable pain.

Suddenly he leaped up, cried aloud, and flung his hands above his head. I thought he was gone this time; but he stopped, poised, as it seemed, over the water, and I heard him cry, "I can't, I can't!" and he sank down all in a heap on the bank, and fell again to sobbing. I hope never to see a man—if you can call Smugg a man—like that again.

He sat where he was, and I where I was, till the moon paled and a distant hint of day discovered us. Then he rose, brushed himself with his hands, and slunk quickly from the bank. Had he looked anywhere but on the ground, he must have seen me; as it was, I only narrowly avoided him, and fell again into my place behind him. All the way back to our garden I followed him. As he passed through the gate, I quickened my pace, overtook him, and laid my hand on his arm. The man's face gave me what I remember my old nurse used to call "quite a turn."

"You're an average idiot, aren't you?" said I. "Oh, yes; I've been squatting in the wet by that infernal river, too. You ought to get three months, by rights."

He looked at me in a dazed sort of way.

"I daren't," he said. "I wanted to, but I daren't."

There is really nothing more. We went to the wedding, leaving Smugg in bed; and in the evening we, leaving Smugg still in bed (I told Mary to keep an eye on him), and carrying a dozen of the grocer's best port, went up to dance at Dill's farm. Joe was polished till I could almost see myself in his cheek, and Pyrrha looked more charming than ever. She and Joe were to leave us early, to go to Joe's own house in the village, but I managed to get one dance with her. Indeed, I believe she wanted a word with me.

"Well, all's well that ends well, isn't it?" I began. "No more scoldings! Not from Mrs. Dill, anyhow."

"You can't let that alone, sir," said Pyrrha.

I chuckled gently.

"Oh, I'll never refer to it again," said I. "This is a fine wedding of yours, Betsy."

"It's good of you and the other gentlemen to come, sir."

"We had to see the last of you," and I sighed very ostentatiously.

Pyrrha laughed. She did not believe in it, and she knew that I knew she did not, but the little compliment pleased her, all the same.

"Smugg," I pursued, "is ill in bed. But perhaps he wouldn't have come, anyhow."

"If you please, sir—" Pyrrha began; but she stopped.

"Yes, Betsy? What is it?"

"Would you take a message for me, sir?"

"If it's a proper one, Betsy, for a married lady to send."

She laughed a little, and said:

"Oh, it's no harm, sir. I'm afraid he aint—he's rather down, sir."

"Who?"

"Why, that Smugg, sir."

"Oh, that Smugg! Why, yes; a little down, Betsy, I fear."

"You might tell him as I bear no malice, sir—as I'm not angry—with him, I mean."

"Certainly," said I. "It will probably do him good."

"He got me into trouble; but there, I can make allowances; and it's all right now, sir."

"In fact you forgive him?"

"I think you might tell him so, sir," said Betsy.

"But," said I, "are you aware that he was another's all the time?"

"What, sir?"

"Oh, yes! engaged to be married."

"Well, I never! Him! What, all the while he—"

"Precisely."

"Well, that beats everything. Oh, if I'd known that!"

"I'll give him your message."

"No, sir, not now, I thank you. The villain!"

"You are right," said I. "I think your mother ought to have—scolded him, too."

"Now you promised, sir—" but Joe came up, and I escaped.

Chapter 4

A Repentant Sinner

It was, I believe, mainly as a compliment to me that Miss Audrey Liston was asked to Poltons. Miss Liston and I were very good friends, and my cousin Dora Polton thought, as she informed me, that it would be nice for me to have someone I could talk to about "books and so on." I did not complain. Miss Liston was a pleasant young woman of six-and-twenty; I liked her very much except on paper, and I was aware that she made it a point of duty to read something at least of what I wrote. She was in the habit of describing herself as an "authoress in a small way." If it were pointed out that six three-volume novels in three years (the term of her literary activity, at the time of which I write) could hardly be called "a small way," she would smile modestly and say that it was not really much; and if she were told that the English language embraced no such word as "authoress," she would smile again and say that it ought to; a position toward the bugbear of correctness with which, I confess, I sympathize in some degree. She was very diligent; she worked from ten to one every day while she was at Poltons; how much she wrote is between her and her conscience.

There was another impeachment which Miss Liston was hardly at the trouble to deny. "Take my characters from life?" she would exclaim. "Surely every artist" (Miss Liston often referred to herself as an artist) "must?" And she would proceed to maintain—what is perhaps true sometimes—that people rather liked being put into books, just as they like being photographed, for all that they grumble and pretend to be afflicted when either process is levied against them. In discussing this matter with Miss Liston I felt myself on delicate ground, for it was notorious that I figured in her first book in the guise of a misogynistic genius; the fact that she lengthened (and thickened) my hair, converted it from an indeterminate brown to a dusky black, gave me a drooping mustache, and invested my very ordinary workaday eyes with a strange magnetic attraction, availed nothing; I was at once recognized; and, I may remark in passing, an uncommonly disagreeable fellow she made me. Thus I had passed through the fire. I felt tolerably sure that I presented no other aspect of interest, real or supposed, and I was quite content that Miss Liston should serve all the rest of her acquaintance as she had served me. I reckoned they would last her, at the present rate of production, about five years.

Fate was kind to Miss Liston, and provided her with most suitable patterns for her next piece of work at Poltons itself. There were a young man and a young woman staying in the house—Sir Gilbert Chillington and Miss Pamela Myles. The moment Miss Liston was apprized of a possible romance, she began the study of the protagonists. She was looking out, she told me, for some new types (if it were any consolation—and there is a sort of dignity about it—to be called a type, Miss Liston's victims were always welcome to so much), and she had found them in Chillington and Pamela. The former appeared to my dull eye to offer no salient novelty; he was tall, broad, handsome, and he possessed a manner of enviable placidity. Pamela, I allowed, was exactly the heroine Miss Liston loved—haughty, capricious, difficile, but sound and true at heart (I was mentally skimming Volume I). Miss Liston agreed with me in my conception of Pamela, but declared that I did not do justice to the artistic possibilities latent in Chillington; he had a curious attraction which it would tax her skill (so she gravely informed me) to the utmost to reproduce. She proposed that I also should make a study of him, and attributed my hurried refusal to a shrinking from the difficulties of the task.

"Of course," she observed, looking at our young friends, who were talking nonsense at the other side of the lawn, "they must have a misunderstanding."

"Why, of course," said I, lighting my pipe. "What should you say to another man?"

"Or another woman?" said Miss Liston.

"It comes to the same thing," said I. (About a volume and a half I meant.)

"But it's more interesting. Do you think she'd better be a married woman?" And Miss Liston looked at me inquiringly.

"The age prefers them married," I remarked.

This conversation happened on the second day of Miss Liston's visit, and she lost no time in beginning to study her subjects. Pamela, she said, she found pretty plain sailing, but Chillington continued to puzzle her. Again, she could not make up her mind whether to have a happy or a tragic ending. In the interests of a tenderhearted public, I pleaded for marriage bells.

"Yes, I think so," said Miss Liston, but she sighed, and I think she had an idea or two for a heart-broken separation, followed by mutual, lifelong, hopeless devotion.

The complexity of young Sir Gilbert did not, in Miss Liston's opinion, appear less on further acquaintance; and indeed, I must admit that she was not altogether wrong in considering him worthy of attention. As I came to know him better, I discerned in him a smothered self-appreciation, which came to light in response to the least tribute of interest or admiration, but was yet far remote from the aggressiveness of a commonplace vanity. In a moment of indiscretion I had chaffed him—he was very good- natured—on the risks he ran at Miss Liston's hands; he was not disgusted, but neither did he plume himself or spread his feathers. He received the suggestion without surprise, and without any attempt at disclaiming fitness for the purpose; but he received it as a matter which entailed a responsibility on him. I detected the conviction that, if the portrait was to be painted, it was due to the world that it should be well painted; the subject must give the artist full opportunities.

"What does she know about me?" he asked, in meditative tones.

"She's very quick; she'll soon pick up as much as she wants," I assured him.

"She'll probably go all wrong," he said somberly; and of course I could not tell him that it was of no consequence if she did. He would not have believed me, and would have done precisely what he proceeded to do, and that was to afford Miss Liston every chance of appraising his character and plumbing the depths of his soul. I may say at once that I did not regret this course of action; for the effect of it was to allow me a chance of talking to Pamela Myles, and Pamela was exactly the sort of girl to beguile the long, pleasant morning hours of a holiday in the country. No one had told Pamela that she was going to be put in a book, and I don't think it would have made any difference had she been told. Pamela's attitude toward books was one of healthy scorn, confidently based on admitted ignorance. So we never spoke of them, and my cousin Dora condoled with me more than once on the way in which Miss Liston, false to the implied terms of her invitation, deserted me in favor of Sir Gilbert, and left me to the mercies of a frivolous girl. Pamela appeared to be as little aggrieved as I was. I imagined that she supposed that Chillington would ask her to marry him some day, before very long, and I was sure she would accept him; but it was quite plain that, if Miss Liston persisted in making Pamela her heroine, she would have to supply from her own resources a large supplement of passion. Pamela was far too deficient in the commodity to be made anything of without such re-enforcement, even by an art more adept at making much out of nothing than Miss Liston's straightforward method could claim to be.

A week passed, and then, one Friday morning, a new light burst on me. Miss Liston came into the garden at eleven o'clock and sat down by me on the lawn. Chillington and Pamela had gone riding with the squire, Dora was visiting the poor. We were alone. The appearance of Miss Liston at this hour (usually sacred to the use of the pen), no less than her puzzled look, told me that an obstruction had occurred in the novel. Presently she let me know what it was.

"I'm thinking of altering the scheme of my story, Mr. Wynne," said she. "Have you ever noticed how sometimes a man thinks he's in love when he isn't really?"

"Such a case sometimes occurs," I acknowledged.

"Yes, and he doesn't find out his mistake—"

"Till they're married?"

"Sometimes, yes," she said, rather as though she were making an unwilling admission. "But sometimes he sees it before—when he meets somebody else."

"Very true," said I, with a grave nod.

"The false can't stand against the real," pursued Miss Liston; and then she fell into meditative silence. I stole a glance at her face; she was smiling. Was it in the pleasure of literary creation—an artistic ecstasy? I should have liked to answer yes, but I doubted it very much. Without pretending to Miss Liston's powers, I have the little subtlety that is needful to show me that more than one kind of smile may be seen on the human face, and that there is one very different from others; and, finally, that that one is not evoked, as a rule, merely by the evolution of the troublesome encumbrance in pretty writing vulgarly called a "plot."

"If," pursued Miss Liston, "someone comes who can appreciate him and draw out what is best in him—"

"That's all very well," said I, "but what of the first girl?"

"Oh, she's—she can be made shallow, you know; and I can put in a man for her. People needn't be much interested in her."

"Yes, you could manage it that way," said I, thinking how Pamela—I took the liberty of using her name for the shallow girl—would like such treatment.

"She will really be valuable mainly as a foil," observed Miss Liston; and she added generously, "I shall make her nice, you know, but shallow—not worthy of him."

"And what are you going to make the other girl like?" I asked.

Miss Liston started slightly; also she colored very slightly, and she answered, looking away from me across the lawn:

"I haven't quite made up my mind yet, Mr. Wynne."

With the suspicion which this conversation aroused fresh in my mind, it was curious to hear Pamela laugh, as she said to me on the afternoon of the same day:

"Aren't Sir Gilbert and Audrey Liston funny? I tell you what, Mr. Wynne, I believe they're writing a novel together."

"Perhaps Chillington's giving her the materials for one," I suggested.

"I shouldn't think," observed Pamela in her dispassionate way, "that anything very interesting had ever happened to him."

"I thought you liked him," I remarked humbly.

"So I do. What's that got to do with it?" asked Pamela.

It was beyond question that Chillington enjoyed Miss Liston's society; the interest she showed in him was incense to his nostrils. I used to overhear fragments of his ideas about himself which he was revealing in answer to her tactful inquiries. But neither was it doubtful that he had by no means lost his relish for Pamela's lighter talk; in fact, he seemed to turn to her with some relief—perhaps it is refreshing to escape from self-analysis, even when the process is conducted in the pleasantest possible manner—and the hours which Miss Liston gave to work were devoted by Chillington to maintaining his cordial relations with the lady whose comfortable and not over-tragical disposal was taxing Miss Liston's skill. For she had definitely decided all her plot—she told me so a few days later.

It was all planned out; nay, the scene in which the truth as to his own feelings bursts on Sir Gilbert (I forget at the moment what name the novel gave him) was, I understood, actually written; the shallow girl was to experience nothing worse than a wound to her vanity, and was to turn, with as much alacrity as decency allowed, to the substitute whom Miss Liston had now provided. All this was poured into my sympathetic ear, and I say sympathetic in all sincerity; for, although I may occasionally treat Miss Liston's literary efforts with less than proper respect, she herself was my friend, and the conviction under which she was now living would, I knew, unless it were justified, bring her into much of that unhappiness in which one generally found her heroine plunged about the end of Volume II. The heroine generally got out all right, and the knowledge that she would enabled the reader to preserve cheerfulness. But would poor little Miss Liston get out? I was none too sure of it.

Suddenly a change came in the state of affairs. Pamela produced it. It must have struck her that the increasing intimacy of Miss Liston and Chillington might become something other than "funny."

To put it briefly and metaphorically, she whistled her dog back to her heels. I am not skilled in understanding or describing the artifices of ladies; but even I saw the transformation in Pamela. She put forth her strength and put on her prettiest gowns; she refused to take her place in the sea-saw of society which Chillington had recently established for his pleasure. If he spent an hour with Miss Liston, Pamela would have nothing of him for a day; she met his attentions with scorn unless they were undivided. Chillington seemed at first puzzled; I believe that he never regarded his talks with Miss Liston in other than a business point of view, but directly he understood that Pamela claimed him, and that she was prepared, in case he did not obey her call, to establish a grievance against him, he lost no time in manifesting his obedience. A whole day passed in which, to my certain knowledge, he was not alone a moment with Miss Liston, and did not, save at the family meals, exchange a word with her. As he walked off with Pamela, Miss Liston's eyes followed him in wistful longing; she stole away upstairs and did not come down till five o'clock. Then, finding me strolling about with a cigarette, she joined me.

"Well, how goes the book?" I asked.

"I haven't done much to it just lately," she answered, in a low voice. "I—it's—I don't quite know what to do with it."

"I thought you'd settled?"

"So I had, but—oh, don't let's talk about it, Mr. Wynne!"

But a moment later she went on talking about it.

"I don't know why I should make it end happily," she said. "I'm sure life isn't always happy, is it?"

"Certainly not," I answered. "You mean your man might stick to the shallow girl after all?"

"Yes," I just heard her whisper.

"And be miserable afterward?" I pursued.

"I don't know," said Miss Liston. "Perhaps he wouldn't."

"Then you must make him shallow himself."

"I can't do that," she said quickly. "Oh, how difficult it is!"

She may have meant merely the art of writing—when I cordially agree with—but I think she meant also the way of the world—which does not make me withdraw my assent. I left her walking up and down in front of the drawing-room windows, a rather forlorn little figure, thrown into distinctness by the cold rays of the setting sun.

All was not over yet. That evening Chillington broke away. Led by vanity, or interest, or friendliness, I know not which—tired may be of paying court (the attitude in which Pamela kept him), and thinking it would be pleasant to play the other part for a while—after dinner he went straight to Miss Liston, talked to her while we had coffee on the terrace, and then walked about with her. Pamela sat by me; she was very silent; she did not appear to be angry, but her handsome mouth wore a resolute expression. Chillington and Miss Liston wandered on into the shrubbery, and did not come into sight again for nearly half an hour.

"I think it's cold," said Pamela, in her cool, quiet tones. "And it's also, Mr. Wynne, rather slow. I shall go to bed."

I thought it a little impertinent of Pamela to attribute the "slowness" (which had undoubtedly existed) to me, so I took my revenge by saying with an assumption of innocence purposely and obviously unreal:

"Oh, but won't you wait and bid Miss Liston and Chillington good-night?"

Pamela looked at me for a moment. I made bold to smile.

Pamela's face broke slowly into an answering smile.

"I don't know what you mean, Mr. Wynne," said she.

"No?" said I.

"No," said Pamela, and she turned away. But before she went she looked over her shoulder, and still smiling, said, "Wish Miss Liston good-night for me, Mr. Wynne. Anything I have to say to Sir Gilbert will wait very well till to-morrow."

She had hardly gone in when the wanderers came out of the shrubbery and rejoined me. Chillington wore his usual passive look, but Miss Liston's face was happy and radiant. Chillington passed on into the drawing room. Miss Liston lingered a moment by me.

"Why, you look," said I, "as if you'd invented the finest scene ever written."

She did not answer me directly, but stood looking up at the stars. Then she said, in a dreamy tone:

"I think I shall stick to my old idea in the book."

As she spoke, Chillington came out. Even in the dim light I saw a frown on his face.

"I say, Wynne," said he, "where's Miss Myles?"

"She's gone to bed," I answered. "She told me to wish you good night for her, Miss Liston. No message for you, Chillington."

Miss Liston's eyes were on him. He took no notice of her; he stood frowning for an instant, then, with some muttered ejaculation, he strode back into the house. We heard his heavy tread across the drawing room; we heard the door slammed behind him, and I found myself looking on Miss Liston's altered face.

"What does he want her for, I wonder!" she said, in an agitation that made my presence, my thoughts, my suspicions, nothing to her. "He said nothing to me about wanting to speak to her to- night." And she walked slowly into the house, her eyes on the ground, and all the light gone from her face, and the joy dead in it. Whereupon I, left alone, began to rail at the gods that a dear, silly little soul like Miss Liston should bother her poor, silly little head about a hulking fool; in which reflections I did, of course, immense injustice not only to an eminent author, but also to a perfectly honorable, though somewhat dense and decidedly conceited, gentleman.

The next morning Sir Gilbert Chillington ate dirt—there is no other way of expressing it—in great quantities and with infinite humility.

My admirable friend Miss Pamela was severe. I saw him walk six yards behind her for the length of the terrace: not a look nor a turn of her head gave him leave to join her. Miss Liston had gone upstairs, and I watched the scene from the window of the smoking room. At last, at the end of the long walk, just where the laurel-bushes mark the beginning of the shrubberies—on the threshold of the scene of his crime—Pamela turned round suddenly and faced the repentant sinner. The most interesting things in life are those which, perhaps by the inevitable nature of the case, one does not hear; and I did not hear the scene which followed. For a while they stood talking—rather, he talked and she listened. Then she turned again and walked slowly into the shrubbery. Chillington followed. It was the end of a chapter, and I laid down the book.

How and from whom Miss Liston heard the news which Chillington himself told me, without a glimmer of shame or a touch of embarrassment, some two hours later, I do not know; but hear it she did before luncheon; for she came down, ready armed with the neatest little speeches for both the happy lovers.

I did not expect Pamela to show an ounce more feeling than the strictest canons of propriety demanded, and she fulfilled my expectations to the letter; but I had hoped, I confess, that Chillington would have displayed some little consciousness. He did not; and it is my belief that, throughout the events which I have recorded, he retained, and that he still retains, the conviction that Miss Liston's interest in him was purely literary and artistic, and that she devoted herself to his society simply because he offered an interesting problem and an inspiring theme.

An ingenious charity may find in that attitude evidence of modesty; to my thinking, it argues a more subtle and magnificent conceit than if he had fathomed the truth, as many humbler men in his place would have done.

On the day after the engagement was accomplished Miss Liston left us to return to London. She came out in her hat and jacket and sat down by me; the carriage was to be round in ten minutes. She put on her gloves slowly and buttoned them carefully. This done, she said:

"By the way, Mr. Wynne, I've adopted your suggestion. The man doesn't find out."

"Then you've made him a fool?" I asked bluntly.

"No," she answered. "I—I think it might happen though he wasn't a fool."

She sat with her hands in her lap for a moment or two, then she went on, in a lower voice:

"I'm going to make him find out afterward."

I felt her glance on me, but I looked straight in front of me.

44

"What, after he's married the shallow girl?"

"Yes," said Miss Liston.

"Rather too late, isn't it? At least, if you mean there is to be a happy ending."

Miss Liston enlaced her fingers.

"I haven't decided about the ending yet," said she.

"If you're intent to be tragical—which is the fashion—you'll do as you stand," said I.

"Yes," she answered slowly, "if I'm tragical, I shall do as I stand."

There was another pause, and rather a long one; the wheels of the carriage were audible on the gravel of the front drive. Miss Liston stood up. I rose and held out my hand.

"Of course," said Miss Liston, still intent on her novel, "I could—" She stopped again, and looked apprehensively at me. My face, I believe, expressed nothing more than polite attention and friendly interest.

"Of course," she began again, "the shallow girl—his wife—might—might die, Mr. Wynne."

"In novels," said I with a smile, "while there's death, there's hope."

"Yes, in novels," she answered, giving me her hand.

The poor little woman was very unhappy. Unwisely, I dare say, I pressed her hand. It was enough, the tears leaped to her eyes; she gave my great fist a hurried squeeze—I have seldom been more touched by any thanks, how ever warm or eloquent—and hurried away.

Chapter 5

'Twixt Will and Will Not

I must confess at once that at first, at least, I very much admired the curate. I am not referring to my admiration of his fine figure—six feet high and straight as an arrow—nor of his handsome, open, ingenuous countenance, or his candid blue eye, or his thick curly hair. No; what won my heart from an early period of my visit to my cousins, the Poltons, of Poltons Park, was the fervent, undisguised, unashamed, confident, and altogether matter-of-course manner in which he made love to Miss Beatrice Queenborough, only daughter and heiress of the wealthy shipowner, Sir Wagstaff Queenborough, Bart., and Eleanor, his wife. It was purely the manner of the curate's advances that took my fancy; in the mere fact of them there was nothing remarkable. For all the men in the house (and a good many outside) made covert, stealthy, and indirect steps in the same direction; for Trix (as her friends called her) was, if not wise, at least pretty and witty, displaying to the material eye a charming figure, and to the mental a delicate heartlessness—both attributes which challenge a self-respecting man's best efforts. But then came the fatal obstacle. From heiresses in reason a gentleman need neither shrink nor let himself be driven; but when it comes to something like twenty thousand a year—the reported amount of Trix's dot—he distrusts his own motives almost as much as the lady's relatives distrust them for him. We all felt this—Stanton, Rippleby, and I; and, although I will not swear that we spoke no tender words and gave no meaning glances, yet we reduced such concessions to natural weakness to a minimum, not only when Lady Queenborough was by, but at all times. To say truth, we had no desire to see our scalps affixed to Miss Trix's pretty belt, nor to have our hearts broken (like that of the young man in the poem) before she went to Homburg in the autumn.

With the curate it was otherwise. He—Jack Ives, by the way, was his name—appeared to rush, not only upon his fate, but in the face of all possibility and of Lady Queenborough. My cousin and hostess, Dora Polton, was very much distressed about him. She said that he was such a nice young fellow, and that it was a great pity to see him preparing such unhappiness for himself. Nay, I happen to know that she spoke very seriously to Trix, pointing out the wickedness of trifling with him; whereupon Trix, who maintained a bowing acquaintance with her conscience, avoided him for a whole afternoon and endangered all Algy Stanton's prudent resolutions by taking him out in the Canadian canoe. This demonstration in no way perturbed the curate. He observed that, as there was nothing better to do, we might as well play billiards, and proceeded to defeat me in three games of a hundred up (no, it is quite immaterial whether we played for anything or not), after which he told Dora that the vicar was taking the evening service—it happened to be the day when there was one at the parish church—a piece of information only relevant in so far as it suggested that Mr. Ives could accept an invitation to dinner if one were proffered him. Dora, very weakly, rose to the bait. Jack Ives, airily remarking that there was no use in ceremony among friends, seized the place next to Trix at dinner (her mother was just opposite) and walked on the terrace after dinner with her in the moonlight. When the ladies retired he came into the smoking room, drank a whisky and soda, said that Miss Queenborough was really a very charming companion, and apologized for leaving us early, on the ground that his sermon was still unwritten. My good cousin, the squire, suggested rather grimly that a discourse on the vanity of human wishes might be appropriate.

"I shall preach," said Mr. Ives thoughtfully, "on the opportunities of wealth."

This resolution he carried out on the next day but one, that being a Sunday. I had the pleasure of sitting next to Miss Trix, and I watched her with some interest as Mr. Ives developed his theme. I will not try to reproduce the sermon, which would have seemed by no means a bad one had any of our party been able to ignore the personal application which we read into it; for its main burden was no other than this—that wealth should be used by those who were fortunate enough to possess it (here Trix looked down and fidgeted with her Prayer-book) as a means of promoting greater union between themselves and the less richly endowed, and not—as, alas! had too often been the case—as though it were a new barrier set up between them and their fellow-creatures (here Miss Trix blushed slightly, and had recourse to her smelling-bottle). "You," said the curate, waxing rhetorical as he addressed an imaginary, but bloated, capitalist, "have no more right to your money than I have. It is intrusted to you to be shared with me." At this point I heard Lady Queenborough sniff and Algy Stanton snigger. I stole a glance at Trix and detected a slight waver in the admirable lines of her mouth.

"A very good sermon, didn't you think?" I said to her, as we walked home.

"Oh, very!" she replied demurely.

"Ah, if we followed all we heard in church!" I sighed.

Miss Trix walked in silence for a few yards. By dint of never becoming anything else, we had become very good friends; and presently she remarked, quite confidentially:

"He's very silly, isn't he?"

"Then you ought to snub him," I said severely.

"So I do—sometimes. He's rather amusing, though."

"Of course, if you're prepared to make the sacrifice involved—"

"Oh, what nonsense!"

"Then you've no business to amuse yourself with him."

"Dear, dear! how moral you are!" said Trix.

The next development in the situation was this: My cousin Dora received a letter from the Marquis of Newhaven, with whom she was acquainted, praying her to allow him to run down to Poltons for a few days; he reminded her that she had once given him a general invitation; if it would not be inconvenient—and so forth. The meaning of this communication did not, of course, escape my cousin, who had witnessed the writer's attentions to Trix in the preceding season, nor did it escape the rest of us (who had talked over the said attentions at the club) when she told us about it, and announced that Lord Newhaven would arrive in the middle of the next day. Trix affected dense unconsciousness; her mother allowed herself a mysterious smile—which, however, speedily vanished when the curate (he was taking lunch with us) observed in a cheerful tone:

"Newhaven! Oh, I remember the chap at the House—plowed twice in Smalls—stumpy fellow, isn't he? Not a bad chap, though, you know, barring his looks. I'm glad he's coming."

"You won't be soon, young man," Lady Queenborough's angry eye seemed to say.

"I remember him," pursued Jack; "awfully smitten with a tobacconist's daughter in the Corn—oh, it's all *right*, Lady Queenborough—she wouldn't look at him."

This quasi apology was called forth by the fact of Lady Queenborough pushing back her chair and making for the door. It did not at all appease her to hear of the scorn of the tobacconist's daughter. She glanced sternly at Jack and disappeared. He turned to Trix and reminded her—without diffidence and coram populo, as his habit was—that she had promised him a stroll in the west wood.

What happened on that stroll I do not know; but meeting Miss Trix on the stairs later in the afternoon, I ventured to remark:

"I hope you broke it to him gently, Miss Queenborough?"

"I don't know what you mean," replied Trix haughtily.

"You were out nearly two hours," said I.

"Were we?" asked Trix, with a start. "Good gracious! Where was mamma, Mr. Wynne?"

"On the lawn—watch in hand."

Miss Trix went slowly upstairs, and there is not the least doubt that something serious passed between her and her mother, for both of them were in the most atrocious of humors that evening. Fortunately, the curate was not there; he had a Bible class.

The next day Lord Newhaven arrived. I found him on the lawn when I strolled up, after a spell of letter-writing, about four o'clock. Lawn tennis was the order of the day, and we were all in flannels.

"Oh, here's Mark!" cried Dora, seeing me. "Now, Mark, you and Mr. Ives had better play against Trix and Lord Newhaven. That'll make a very good set."

"No, no, Mrs. Polton," said Jack Ives. "They wouldn't have a chance. Look here, I'll play with Miss Queenborough against Lord Newhaven and Wynne."

Newhaven—whose appearance, by the way, though hardly distinguished, was not quite so unornamental as the curate had led us to expect—looked slightly displeased, but Jack gave him no time for remonstrance. He whisked Trix off and began to serve all in a moment. I had a vision of Lady Queenborough approaching from the house with face aghast. The set went on; and, owing entirely to Newhaven's absurd chivalry in sending all the balls to Jack Ives instead of following the well-known maxim to "pound away at the lady," they beat us. Jack wiped his brow, strolled up to the tea table with Trix, and remarked in exultant tones:

"We make a perfect couple, Miss Queenborough; we ought never to be separated."

Dora did not ask the curate to dinner that night, but he dropped in about nine o'clock to ask her opinion as to the hymns on Sunday; and finding Miss Trix and Newhaven in the small drawing room, he sat down and talked to them. This was too much for Trix; she had treated him very kindly and had allowed him to amuse her; but it was impossible to put up with presumption of that kind. Difficult as it was to discourage Mr. Ives, she did it, and he went away with a disconsolate, puzzled expression. At the last moment, however, Trix so far relented as to express a hope that he was coming to tennis to-morrow, at which he brightened up a little. I do not wish to be uncharitable—least of all to a charming young lady—-but my opinion is that Miss Trix did not wish to set the curate altogether adrift. I think, however, that Lady Queenborough must have spoken again, for when Jack did come to tennis, Trix treated him with most freezing civility and a hardly disguised disdain, and devoted herself to

Lord Newhaven with as much assiduity as her mother could wish. We men, over our pipes, expressed the opinion that Jack Ives' little hour of sunshine was past, and that nothing was left to us but to look on at the prosperous, uneventful course of Lord Newhaven's wooing. Trix had had her fun (so Algy Stanton bluntly phrased it) and would now settle down to business.

"I believe, though," he added, "that she likes the curate a bit, you know."

During the whole of the next day—Wednesday—Jack Ives kept away; he had, apparently, accepted the inevitable, and was healing his wounded heart by a strict attention to his parochial duties. Newhaven remarked on his absence with an air of relief, and Miss Trix treated it as a matter of no importance; Lady Queenborough was all smiles; and Dora Polton restricted herself to exclaiming, as I sat by her at tea, in a low tone and a propos of nothing in particular, "Oh, well—poor Mr. Ives!"

But on Thursday there occurred an event, the significance of which passed at the moment unperceived, but which had, in fact, most important results. This was no other than the arrival of little Mrs. Wentworth, an intimate friend of Dora's. Mrs. Wentworth had been left a widow early in life; she possessed a comfortable competence; she was not handsome, but she was vivacious, amusing, and, above all, sympathetic. She sympathized at once with Lady Queenborough in her maternal anxieties, with Trix on her charming romance, with Newhaven on his sweet devotedness, with the rest of us in our obvious desolation—and, after a confidential chat with Dora, she sympathized most strongly with poor Mr. Ives on his unfortunate attachment. Nothing would satisfy her, so Dora told me, except the opportunity of plying Mr. Ives with her soothing balm; and Dora was about to sit down and write him a note, when he strolled in through the drawing room window, and announced that his cook's mother was ill, and that he should be very much obliged if Mrs. Polton would give him some dinner that evening. Trix and Newhaven happened to enter by the door at the same moment, and Jack darted up to them, and shook hands with the greatest effusion. He had evidently buried all unkindness—and with it, we hoped, his mistaken folly. However

52

that might be, he made no effort to engross Trix, but took his seat most docilely by his hostess—and she, of course, introduced him to Mrs. Wentworth. His behavior was, in fact, so exemplary that even Lady Queenborough relaxed her severity, and condescended to cross-examine him on the morals and manners of the old women of the parish. "Oh, the vicar looks after them," said Jack; and he turned to Mrs. Wentworth again.

There can be no doubt that Mrs. Wentworth had a remarkable power of sympathy. I took her in to dinner, and she was deep in the subject of my "noble and inspiring art" before the soup was off the table. Indeed, I'm sure that my life's ambitions would have been an open book to her by the time that the joint arrived, had not Jack Ives, who was sitting on the lady's other side, cut into the conversation just as Mrs. Wentworth was comparing my early struggles with those of Mr. Carlyle. After this intervention of Jack's I had not a chance. I ate my dinner without the sauce 'of sympathy, substituting for it a certain amusement which I derived from studying the face of Miss Trix Queenborough, who was placed on the opposite side of the table. And if Trix did look now and again at Mrs. Wentworth and Jack Ives, I cannot say that her conduct was unnatural. To tell the truth, Jack was so obviously delighted with his new friend that it was quite pleasant—and, as I say, under the circumstances, rather amusing—to watch them. We felt that the squire was justified in having a hit at Jack when Jack said, in the smoking room, that he found himself rather at a loss for a subject for his next sermon.

"What do you say," suggested my cousin, puffing at his pipe, "to taking constancy as your text?"

Jack considered the idea for a moment, but then he shook his head.

"No. I think," he said reflectively, "that I shall preach on the power of sympathy."

That sermon afforded me—I must confess it, at the risk of seeming frivolous—very great entertainment. Again I secured a place by Miss Trix—on her left, Newhaven being on her right, and her face was worth study when Jack Ives gave us a most eloquent description of the wonderful gift in question. It was, he said, the essence and the crown of true womanliness, and it showed itself—well, to put it quite plainly, it showed itself, according to Jack Ives, in exactly that sort of manner and bearing which so honorably and gracefully distinguished Mrs. Wentworth. The lady was not, of course, named, but she was clearly indicated. "Your gift, your precious gift," cried the curate, apostrophizing the impersonation of sympathy, "is given to you, not for your profit, but for mine. It is yours, but it is a trust to be used for me. It is yours, in fact, to share with me." At this climax, which must have struck upon her ear with a certain familiarity, Miss Trix Queenborough, notwithstanding the place and occasion, tossed her pretty head and whispered to me, "What horrid stuff!"

In the ensuing week Jack Ives was our constant companion; the continued illness of his servant's mother left him stranded, and Dora's kind heart at once offered him the hospitality of her roof. For my part I was glad, for the little drama which now began was not without its interest. It was a pleasant change to see Jack genially polite to Trix Queenborough, but quite indifferent to her presence or absence, and content to allow her to take Newhaven for her partner at tennis as often as she pleased. He himself was often an absentee from our games. Mrs. Wentworth did not play, and Jack would sit under the trees with her, or take her out in the canoe. What Trix thought I did not know, but it is a fact that she treated poor Newhaven like dirt beneath her feet, and that Lady Queenborough's face began to lose its transiently pleasant expression. I had a vague idea that a retribution was working itself out, and disposed myself to see the process with all the complacency induced by the spectacle of others receiving punishment for their sins.

A little scene which occurred after lunch one day was significant. I was sitting on the terrace, ready booted and breeched, waiting for my horse to be brought round. Trix came out and sat down by me.

"Where's Newhaven?" I asked.

"Oh, I don't always want Lord Newhaven!" she exclaimed petulantly. "I sent him off for a walk—I'm going out in the Canadian canoe with Mr. Ives."

"Oh, you are, are you?" said I, smiling. As I spoke, Jack Ives ran up to us.

"I say, Miss Queenborough," he cried, "I've just got your message saying you'd let me take you on the lake."

"Is it a great bore?" asked Trix, with a glance—a glance that meant mischief.

"I should like it awfully, of course," said Jack; "but the fact is I've promised to take Mrs. Wentworth—before I got your message, you know."

Trix drew herself up.

"Of course, if Mrs. Wentworth—" she began.

"I'm very sorry," said Jack.

Then Miss Queenborough, forgetting—as I hope—or choosing to disregard my presence, leaned forward and asked, in her most coaxing tones:

"Don't you ever forget a promise, Mr. Ives?"

Jack looked at her. I suppose her dainty prettiness struck him afresh, for he wavered and hesitated.

"She's gone upstairs," pursued the tempter, "and we shall be safe away before she comes down again."

Jack shuffled with one foot on the gravel.

"I tell you what," he said; "I'll ask her if she minds me taking you for a little while before I—"

I believe he really thought that he had hit upon a compromise satisfactory to all parties. If so, he was speedily undeceived. Trix flushed red and answered angrily:

"Pray don't trouble. I don't want to go."

"Perhaps afterward you might," suggested the curate, but now rather timidly.

"I'm going out with Lord Newhaven," said she. And she added, in an access of uncontrollable annoyance. "Go, please go. I—I don't want you."

Jack sheered off, with a look of puzzled shamefacedness. He disappeared into the house. Nothing passed between Miss Trix and myself. A moment later Newhaven came out.

"Why, Miss Queenborough," said he, in apparent surprise, "Ives is going with Mrs. Wentworth in the canoe!"

In an instant I saw what she had done. In rash presumption she had told Newhaven that she was going with the curate—and now the curate had refused to take her—and Ives had met him in search of Mrs. Wentworth. What could she do? Well, she rose—or fell—to the occasion. In the coldest of voices she said;

"I thought you'd gone for your walk."

"I was just starting," he answered apologetically, "when I met Ives. But, as you weren't going with him—" He paused, an inquiring look in his eyes. He was evidently asking himself why she had not gone with the curate.

"I'd rather be left alone, if you don't mind," said she. And then, flushing red again, she added. "I changed my mind and refused to go with Mr. Ives. So he went off to get Mrs. Wentworth instead."

I started. Newhaven looked at her for an instant, and then turned on his heel. She turned to me, quick as lightning, and with her face all aflame.

"If you tell, I'll never speak to you again," she whispered.

After this there was silence for some minutes.

"Well?" she said, without looking at me.

"I have no remark to offer, Miss Queenborough," I returned.

"I suppose that was a lie, wasn't it?" she asked defiantly.

"It's not my business to say what it was," was my discreet answer.

"I know what you're thinking."

"I was thinking," said I, "which I would rather be—the man you will marry, or the man you would like—"

"How dare you! It's not true. Oh Mr. Wynne, indeed it's not true!"

Whether it were true or not I did not know. But if it had been, Miss Trix Queenborough might have been expected to act very much in the way in which she proceeded to act: that is to say, to be extravagantly attentive to Lord Newhaven when Jack Ives was present, and markedly neglectful of him in the curate's absence. It also fitted in very well with the theory which I had ventured to hint that her bearing toward Mrs. Wentworth was distinguished by a stately civility, and her remarks about that lady by a superfluity of laudation; for if these be not two distinguishing marks of rivalry in the well-bred, I must go back to my favorite books and learn from them—more folly.

And if Trix's manners were all that they should be, praise no less high must be accorded to Mrs. Wentworth's; she attained an altitude of admirable unconsciousness and conducted her flirtation (the poverty of language forces me to the word, but it is over- flippant) with the curate in a staid, quasi-maternal way. She called him a delightful boy, and said that she was intensely interested in all his aims and hopes.

"What does she want?" I asked Dora despairingly. "She can't want to marry him." I was referring to Trix Queenborough, not to Mrs. Wentworth.

"Good gracious, no!" answered Dora, irritably. "It's simple jealousy. She won't let the poor boy alone till he's in love with her again. It's a horrible shame!"

"Oh, well, he has great recuperative power," said I.

"She'd better be careful, though. It's a very dangerous game. How do you suppose Lord Newhaven likes it?"

Accident gave me that very day a hint how little Lord Newhaven liked it, and a glimpse of the risk Miss Trix was running. Entering the library suddenly, I heard Newhaven's voice raised above his ordinary tones.

"I won't stand it!" he was declaring. "I never know how she'll treat me from one minute to the next."

My entrance, of course, stopped the conversation very abruptly. Newhaven had come to a stand in the middle of the room, and Lady Queenborough sat on the sofa, a formidable frown on her brow. Withdrawing myself as rapidly as possible, I argued the probability of a severe lecture for Miss Trix, ending in a command to try her noble suitor's patience no longer. I hope all this happened, for I, not seeing why Mrs. Wentworth should monopolize the grace of sympathy, took the liberty of extending mine to Newhaven. He was certainly in love with Trix, not with her money, and the treatment he underwent must have been as trying to his feelings as it was galling to his pride.

My sympathy was not premature, for Miss Trix's fascinations, which were indubitably great, began to have their effect. The scene about the canoe was re-enacted, but with a different denouement. This time the promise was forgotten, and the widow forsaken. Then Mrs. Wentworth put on her armor. We had, in fact, reached this very absurd situation, that these two ladies were contending for the favors of, or the domination over, such an obscure, poverty-stricken, hopelessly ineligible person as the curate of Poltons undoubtedly was. The position seemed to me then, and still seems, to indicate some remarkable qualities in that young man.

At last Newhaven made a move. At breakfast, on Wednesday morning, he announced that, reluctant as he should be to leave Poltons Park, he was due at his aunt's place, in Kent, on Saturday evening, and must, therefore, make his arrangements to leave by noon on that day. The significance was apparent. Had he come down to breakfast with "Now or Never!" stamped in fiery letters across his brow, it would have been more obtrusive, indeed, but not a whit plainer. We all looked down at our plates, except Jack Ives. He flung one glance (I saw it out of the corner of my left eye) at Newhaven, another at Trix; then he remarked kindly:

"We shall be uncommonly sorry to lose you, Newhaven."

Events began to happen now, and I will tell them as well as I am able, supplementing my own knowledge by what I learned afterward from Dora—she having learned it from the actors in the scene. In spite of the solemn warning conveyed in Newhaven's intimation, Trix, greatly daring, went off immediately after lunch for what she described as "a long ramble" with Mr. Ives. There was, indeed, the excuse of an old woman at the end of the ramble, and Trix provided Jack with a small basket of comforts for the useful old body; but the ramble was, we felt, the thing, and I was much annoyed at not being able to accompany the walkers in the cloak of darkness or other invisible contrivance. The ramble consumed three hours—full measure. Indeed, it was half-past six before Trix, alone, walked up the drive. Newhaven, a solitary figure, paced up and down the terrace fronting the drive. Trix came on, her head thrown back and a steady smile on her lips. She saw Newhaven; he stood looking at her for a moment with what she afterward described as an indescribable smile on his face, but not, as Dora understood from her, by any means a pleasant one. Yet, if not pleasant, there is not the least doubt in the world that it was highly significant, for she cried out nervously: "Why are you looking at me like that? What's the matter?"

Newhaven, still saying nothing, turned his back on her, and made as if he would walk into the house and leave her there, ignored, discarded, done with. She, realizing the crisis which had come, forgetting everything except the imminent danger of losing him once for all, without time for long explanation or any round- about seductions, ran forward, laying her hand on his arm and blurting out:

"But I've refused him."

I do not know what Newhaven thinks now, but I sometimes doubt whether he would not have been wiser to shake off the detaining hand, and pursue his lonely way, first into the house, and ultimately to his aunt's. But (to say nothing of the twenty thousand a year, which, after all, and be you as romantic as you may please to be, is not a thing to be sneezed at) Trix's face, its mingled eagerness and shame, its flushed cheeks and shining eyes, the piquancy of its unwonted humility, overcame him. He stopped dead.

"I—I was obliged to give him an—an opportunity," said Miss Trix, having the grace to stumble a little in her speech. "And—and it's all your fault."

The war was thus, by happy audacity, carried into Newhaven's own quarters.

"My fault!" he exclaimed. "My fault that you walk all day with that curate!"

Then Miss Trix—and let no irrelevant considerations mar the appreciation of fine acting—dropped her eyes and murmured softly:

"I—I was so terribly afraid of seeming to expect *you.*"

Wherewith she (and not he) ran away lightly up the stairs, turning just one glance downward as she reached the landing. Newhaven was looking up from below with an "enchanted" smile—the word is Trix's own; I should probably have used a different one.

Was then the curate of Poltons utterly defeated—brought to his knees, only to be spurned? It seemed so; and he came down to dinner that night with a subdued and melancholy expression. Trix, on the other hand, was brilliant and talkative to the last degree, and the gayety spread from her all around the table, leaving untouched only the rejected lover and Mrs. Wentworth; for the last named lady, true to her distinguishing quality, had begun to talk to poor Jack Ives in low, soothing tones.

After dinner Trix was not visible; but the door of the little boudoir beyond stood half-open, and very soon Newhaven edged his way through. Almost at the same moment Jack Ives and Mrs. Wentworth passed out of the window and began to walk up and down the gravel. Nobody but myself appeared to notice these remarkable occurrences, but I watched them with keen interest. Half an hour passed, and then there smote on my watchful ear the sound of a low laugh from the boudoir. It was followed almost immediately by a stranger sound from the gravel walk. Then, all in a moment, two things happened. The boudoir door opened, and Trix, followed by Newhaven, came in, smiling; from the window entered Jack Ives and Mrs. Wentworth. My eyes were on the curate. He gave one sudden, comprehending glance toward the other couple; then he took the widow's hand, led her up to Dora, and said, in low yet penetrating tones.

"Will you wish us joy, Mrs. Polton?"

The squire, Rippleby, and Algy Stanton were round them in an instant. I kept my place, watching now the face of Trix Queenborough. She turned first flaming red, then very pale. I saw her turn to Newhaven and speak one or two urgent, imperative words to him. Then, drawing herself up to her full height, she crossed the room to where the group was assembled round Mrs. Wentworth and Jack Ives.

"What's the matter? What are you saying?" she asked.

Mrs. Wentworth's eyes were modestly cast down, but a smile played round her mouth. No one spoke for a moment. Then Jack Ives said:

"Mrs. Wentworth has promised to be my wife, Miss Queenborough."

For a moment, hardly perceptible, Trix hesitated; then, with the most winning, touching, sweetest smile in the world, she said:

"So you took my advice, and our afternoon walk was not wasted, after all?"

Mrs. Polton is not used to these fine flights of diplomacy; she had heard before dinner something of what had actually happened in the afternoon; and the simple woman positively jumped. Jack Ives met Trix's scornful eyes full and square.

"Not at all wasted," said he, with a smile. "Not only has it shown me where my true happiness lies, but it has also given me a juster idea of the value and sincerity of your regard for me, Miss Queenborough."

"It is as real, Mr. Ives, as it is sincere," said she.

"It is like yourself, Miss Queenborough," said he, with a little bow; and he turned from her and began to talk to his fiancee.

Trix Queenborough moved slowly toward where I sat. Newhaven was watching her from where he stood alone on the other side of the room.

"And have you no news for us?" I asked in low tones.

"Thank you," she said haughtily; "I don't care that mine should be a pendent to the great tidings about the little widow and curate."

After a moment's pause she went on:

"He lost no time, did he? He was wise to secure her before what happened this afternoon could leak out. Nobody can tell her now."

"This afternoon?"

"He asked me to marry him this afternoon."

"And you refused?"

"Yes."

"Well, his behavior is in outrageously bad taste, but—"

She laid a hand on my arm, and said in calm, level tones.

"I refused him because I dared not have him; but I told him I cared for him, and he said he loved me. And I let him kiss me. Good-night, Mr. Wynne."

I sat still and silent. Newhaven came across to us. Trix put up her hand and caught him by the sleeve.

"Fred," she said, "my dear, honest old Fred; you love me, don't you?"

Newhaven, much embarrassed and surprised, looked at me in alarm. But her hand was in his now, and her eyes imploring him.

"I should rather think I did, my dear," said he.

I really hope that Lord and Lady Newhaven will not be very unhappy, while Mrs. Ives quite worships her husband, and is convinced that she eclipsed the brilliant and wealthy Miss Queenborough.

Perhaps she did—perhaps not.

There are, as I have said, great qualities in the curate of Poltons, but I have not quite made up my mind precisely what they are. I ought, however, to say that Dora takes a more favorable view of him and a less lenient view of Trix than I.

That is perhaps natural. Besides, Dora does not know the precise manner in which the curate was refused. By the way, he preached next Sunday on the text, "The children of this world are wiser in their generation than the children of light."

Chapter 6

Which Shall It Be?

It was a charmingly mild and balmy day. The sun shone beyond the orchard, and the shade was cool inside. A light breeze stirred the boughs of the old apple tree under which the philosopher sat.

None of these things did the philosopher notice, unless it might be when the wind blew about the leaves of the large volume on his knees, and he had to find his place again. Then he would exclaim against the wind, shuffle the leaves till he got the right page, and settle to his reading. The book was a treatise on ontology; it was written by another philosopher, a friend of this philosopher's; it bristled with fallacies, and this philosopher was discovering them all, and noting them on the fly leaf at the end. He was not going to review the book (as some might have thought from his behavior), or even to answer it in a work of his own. It was just that he found a pleasure in stripping any poor fallacy naked and crucifying it.

Presently a girl in a white frock came into the orchard. She picked up an apple, bit it, and found it ripe. Holding it in her hand she walked up to where the philosopher sat, and looked at him. He did not stir. She took a bite out of the apple, munched it, and swallowed it. The philosopher crucified a fallacy on the fly leaf. The girl flung the apple away.

"Mr. Jerningham," said she, "are you very busy?"

The philosopher, pencil in hand, looked up.

"No, Miss May," said he, "not very."

"Because I want your opinion."

"In one moment," said the philosopher apologetically.

He turned back to the fly leaf and began to nail the last fallacy a little tighter to the cross. The girl regarded him, first with amused impatience, then with a vexed frown, finally with a wistful regret. He was so very old for his age, she thought; he could not be much beyond thirty; his hair was thick and full of waves, his eyes bright and clear, his complexion not yet divested of all youth's relics.

"Now, Miss May, I am at your service," said the philosopher, with a lingering look at his impaled fallacy. And he closed the book, keeping it, however, on his knee.

The girl sat down just opposite to him.

"It's a very important thing I want to ask you," she began, tugging at a tuft of grass, "and it's very—difficult, and you mustn't tell anyone I asked you; at least, I'd rather you didn't."

"I shall not speak of it; indeed, I shall probably not remember it," said the philosopher.

"And you mustn't look at me, please, while I'm asking you."

"I don't think I was looking at you, but if I was I beg your pardon," said the philosopher apologetically.

She pulled the tuft of grass right out of the ground and flung it from her with all her force.

"Suppose a man—" she began. "No, that's not right."

"You can take any hypothesis you please," observed the philosopher, "but you must verify it afterward, of course."

"Oh, do let me go on. Suppose a girl, Mr. Jerningham—I wish you wouldn't nod."

"It was only to show that I followed you."

"Oh, of course you 'follow me,' as you call it. Suppose a girl had two lovers—you're nodding again—or, I ought to say, suppose there were two men who might be in love with a girl."

"Only two?" asked the philosopher. "You see, any number of men *might* be in love with—"

"Oh, we can leave the rest out," said Miss May, with a sudden dimple; "they don't matter."

"Very well," said the philosopher. "If they are irrelevant, we will put them aside."

"Suppose, then, that one of these men was—oh, *awfully* in love with the girl—and—and proposed, you know—"

"A moment!" said the philosopher, opening a notebook. "Let me take down his proposition. What was it?"

"Why, proposed to her—asked her to marry him," said the girl, with a stare.

"Dear me! How stupid of me! I forgot that special use of the word. Yes?"

"The girl likes him pretty well, and her people approve of him and all that, you know."

"That simplifies the problem," said the philosopher, nodding again.

"But she's not in—in love with him, you know. She doesn't *really* care for him—*much*. Do you understand?"

"Perfectly. It is a most natural state of mind."

"Well, then, suppose that there's another man—what are you writing?"

"I only put down (B.)—like that," pleaded the philosopher, meekly exhibiting his notebook.

She looked at him in a sort of helpless exasperation, with just a smile somewhere in the background of it.

"Oh, you really are—" she exclaimed. "But let me go on. The other man is a friend of the girl's; he's very clever—oh, fearfully clever; and he's rather handsome. You needn't put that down."

"It is certainly not very material," admitted the philosopher, and he crossed out "handsome." "Clever" he left.

"And the girl is most awfully—she admires him tremendously; she thinks him just the greatest man that ever lived, you know. And she—she—" The girl paused.

"I'm following," said the philosopher, with pencil poised.

"She'd think it better than the whole world if—if she could be anything to him, you know."

"You mean become his wife?"

"Well, of course I do—at least suppose I do."

"You spoke rather vaguely, you know."

The girl cast one glance at the philosopher as she replied:

"Well, yes. I did mean, become his wife."

"Yes. Well?"

"But," continued the girl, starting on another tuft of grass, "he doesn't think much about those things. He likes her. I think he likes her—"

"Well, doesn't dislike her?" suggested the philosopher. "Shall we call him indifferent?"

"I don't know. Yes, rather indifferent. I don't think he thinks about it, you know. But she—she's pretty. You needn't put that down."

"I was not about to do so," observed the philosopher.

"She thinks life with him would be just heaven; and—and she thinks she would make him awfully happy. She would—would be so proud of him, you see."

"I see. Yes!"

"And—I don't know how to put it, quite—she thinks that, if he ever thought about it all, he might care for her; because he doesn't care for anybody else; and she's pretty—"

"You said that before."

"Oh, dear! I dare say I did. And most men care for somebody, don't they? Some girl, I mean."

"Most men, no doubt," conceded the philosopher.

"Well, then, what ought she to do? It's not a real thing, you know, Mr. Jerningham. It's in—in a novel I was reading." She said this hastily, and blushed as she spoke.

"Dear me! And it's quite an interesting case! Yes, I see. The question is, Will she act most wisely in accepting the offer of the man who loves her exceedingly, but for whom she entertains only a moderate affection—"

"Yes. Just a liking. He's just a friend."

"Exactly. Or in marrying the other, whom she loves ex—"

"That's not it. How can she marry him? He hasn't—he hasn't asked her, you see."

"True. I forgot. Let us assume, though, for the moment, that he has asked her. She would then have to consider which marriage would probably be productive of the greater sum total of—"

"Oh, but you needn't consider that."

"But it seems the best logical order. We can afterward make allowance for the element of uncertainty caused by—"

"Oh, no! I don't want it like that. I know perfectly well which she'd do if he—the other man, you know—asked her."

"You apprehend that—"

"Never mind what I 'apprehend.' Take it just as I told you."

"Very good. A has asked her hand, B has not."

"Yes."

"May I take it that, but for the disturbing influence of B, A would be a satisfactory—er—candidate?"

"Ye—es. I think so."

"She, therefore, enjoys a certainty of considerable happiness if she marries A?"

"Ye—es. Not perfect, because of—B, you know."

"Quite so, quite so; but still a fair amount of happiness. Is it not so?"

"I don't—well, perhaps."

"On the other hand, if B did ask her, we are to postulate a higher degree of happiness for her?"

"Yes, please, Mr. Jerningham—much higher."

"For both of them?"

"For her. Never mind him."

"Very well. That again simplifies the problem. But his asking her is a contingency only?"

"Yes, that's all."

The philosopher spread out his hands.

"My dear young lady," he said, "it becomes a question of degree. How probable or improbable is it?"

"I don't know. Not very probable—unless—unless—"

"Well?"

"Unless he did happen to notice, you know."

"Ah, yes. We supposed that, if he thought of it, he would probably take the desired step—at least that he might be led to do so. Could she not—er—indicate her preference?"

"She might try—no, she couldn't do much. You see, he—he doesn't think about such things."

"I understand precisely. And it seems to me, Miss May, that in that very fact we find our solution."

"Do we?" she asked.

"I think so. He has evidently no natural inclination toward her—perhaps not toward marriage at all. Any feeling aroused in him would be necessarily shallow and in a measure artificial—and in all likelihood purely temporary. Moreover, if she took steps to arouse his attention, one of two things would be likely to happen. Are you following me?"

"Yes, Mr. Jerningham."

"Either he would be repelled by her overtures—which you must admit is not improbable—and then the position would be unpleasant, and even degrading, for her. Or, on the other hand, he might, through a misplaced feeling of gallantry—"

"Through what?"

"Through a mistaken idea of politeness, or a mistaken view of what was kind, allow himself to be drawn into a connection for which he had no genuine liking. You agree with me that one or other of these things would be likely?"

"Yes, I suppose they would, unless he did come to care for her."

"Ah, you return to that hypothesis. I think it's an extremely fanciful one. No. She needn't marry A, but she must let B alone."

The philosopher closed his book, took off his glasses, wiped them, replaced them, and leaned back against the trunk of the apple tree. The girl picked a dandelion in pieces. After a long pause she asked:

"You think B's feelings wouldn't be at all likely to—to change?"

"That depends on the sort of man he is. But if he is an able man, with intellectual interests which engross him—a man who has chosen his path in life—a man to whom women's society is not a necessity—"

"He's just like that," said the girl, and she bit the head off a daisy.

"Then," said the philosopher, "I see not the least reason for supposing that his feelings will change."

"And would you advise her to marry the other—A?"

"Well, on the whole, I should. A is a good fellow (I think we made A a good fellow); he is a suitable match; his love for her is true and genuine—"

"It's tremendous!"

"Yes—and—er—extreme. She likes him. There is every reason to hope that her liking will develop into a sufficiently deep and stable affection. She will get rid of her folly about B and make A a good wife. Yes, Miss May, if I were the author of your novel, I should make her marry A, and I should call that a happy ending."

A silence followed. It was broken by the philosopher.

"Is that all you wanted my opinion about, Miss May?" he asked, with his finger between the leaves of the treatise on ontology.

"Yes, I think so. I hope I haven't bored you?"

"I've enjoyed the discussion extremely. I had no idea that novels raised points of such psychological interest. I must find time to read one."

The girl had shifted her position till, instead of her full face, her profile was turned toward him. Looking away toward the paddock that lay brilliant in sunshine on the skirts of the apple orchard, she asked, in low, slow tones, twisting her hands in her lap:

"Don't you think that perhaps, if B found out afterward—when she had married A, you know—that she had cared for him so very, very much, he might be a little sorry?"

"If he were a gentleman, he would regret it deeply."

"I mean—sorry on his own account; that—that he had thrown away all that, you know?"

The professor looked meditative.

"I think," he pronounced, "that it is very possible he would. I can well imagine it."

"He might never find anybody to love him like that again," she said, gazing on the gleaming paddock.

"He probably would not," agreed the philosopher.

"And—and most people like being loved, don't they?"

"To crave for love is an almost universal instinct, Miss May."

"Yes, almost," she said, with a dreary little smile. "You see, he'll get old and—and have no one to look after him."

"He will."

"And no home."

"Well, in a sense none," corrected the philosopher, smiling. "But really, you'll frighten me. I'm a bachelor myself, you know, Miss May."

"Yes," she whispered just audibly.

"And all your terrors are before me."

"Well, unless—"

"Oh, we needn't have that 'unless,'" laughed the philosopher cheerfully. "There's no 'unless' about it, Miss May."

The girl jumped to her feet; for an instant she looked at the philosopher. She opened her lips as if to speak, and, at the thought of what lay at her tongue's tip, her face grew red. But the philosopher was gazing past her, and his eyes rested in calm contemplation on the gleaming paddock.

"A beautiful thing, sunshine, to be sure," said he.

Her blush faded away into paleness; her lips closed. Without speaking she turned and walked slowly away, her head drooping. The philosopher heard the rustle of her skirt in the long grass of the orchard; he watched her for a few moments.

"A pretty, graceful creature," said he, with a smile. Then he opened his book, took his pencil in his hand, and slipped in a careful forefinger to mark the fly leaf.

The sun had passed mid-heaven, and began to decline westward before he finished the book. Then he stretched himself and looked at his watch.

"Good gracious, two o'clock! I shall be late for lunch!" and he hurried to his feet.

He was very late for lunch.

"Everything's cold," wailed his hostess. "Where have you been, Mr. Jerningham?"

"Only in the orchard—reading."

"And you've missed May!"

"Missed Miss May? How do you mean? I had a long talk with her this morning—a most interesting talk."

"But you weren't here to say goodby. Now, you don't mean to say that you forgot that she was leaving by the two o'clock train? What a man you are!"

"Dear me! To think of my forgetting it!" said the philosopher shamefacedly.

"She told me to say good-by to you for her."

"She's very kind. I can't forgive myself."

His hostess looked at him for a moment; then she sighed, and smiled, and sighed again.

"Have you everything you want?" she asked.

"Everything, thank you," said he, sitting down opposite the cheese, and propping his book (he thought he would just run through the last chapter again) against the loaf; "everything in the world that I want, thanks."

His hostess did not tell him that the girl had come in from the apple orchard, and run hastily upstairs lest her friend should see what her friend did see in her eyes. So that he had no suspicion at all that he had received an offer of marriage—and refused it. And he did not refer to anything of that sort when he paused once in his reading and exclaimed:

"I'm really sorry I missed Miss May. That was an interesting case of hers. But I gave the right answer. The girl ought to marry A."

And so the girl did.

Chapter 7

Marriage by Compulsion

It is a most anxious thing to be an absolute ruler," said Duke Deodonato, "but I have made up my mind. The Doctor has convinced me [here Dr. Fusbius, Ph. D., bowed very low] that marriage is the best, noblest, wholesomest, and happiest of human conditions."

"Your Highness will remember—" began the President of the Council.

"My lord, I have made up my mind," said Duke Deodonato.

Thus speaking, the Duke took a large sheet of foolscap paper, and wrote rapidly for a moment or two.

"There," he said, pushing the paper over to the President, "is the decree."

"The decree, sir?"

"I think three weeks afford ample space," said Duke Deodonato.

"Three weeks, sir?"

"For every man over twenty-one years of age in this Duchy to find himself a wife."

"Your Highness," observed Dr. Fusbius, with deference, "will consider that between an abstract proposition and a practical measure—"

"There is to the logical mind no stopping place," interrupted Duke Deodonato.

"But, sir," cried the President, "imagine the consternation which this—"

"Let it be gazetted to-night," said Duke Deodonato.

"I would venture," said the President, "to remind your Highness that you are yourself a bachelor."

"Laws," said Duke Deodonato, "do not bind the Crown unless the Crown is expressly mentioned."

"True, sir; but I humbly conceive that it would be pessimi exempli—"

"You are right; I will marry myself," said Duke Deodonato.

"But, sir, three weeks! The hand of a princess cannot be requested and granted in—"

"Then find me somebody else," said Deodonato; "and pray leave me.

I would be alone;" and Duke Deodonato waved his hand to the door.

Outside the door the President said to the Doctor:

"I could wish, sir, that you had not convinced his Highness."

"My lord," rejoined the Doctor, "truth is my only preoccupation."

"Sir," said the President, "are you married?"

"My lord," answered the Doctor, "I am not."

"I thought not," said the President, as he folded up the decree and put it in his pocket.

It is useless to deny that Duke Deodonato's decree caused considerable disturbance in the Duchy. In the first place, the Crown lawyers raised a puzzle of law. Did the word "man" as used in the decree, include "woman"? The President shook his head, and referred the question to his Highness.

"It seems immaterial," observed the Duke. "If a man marries, a woman marries."

"Ex vi terminorum," assented the Doctor.

"But, sir," said the President, "there are more women than men in the Duchy."

Duke Deodonato threw down his pen.

"This is very provoking," said he. "Why was it allowed? I'm sure it happened before _I_ came to the throne."

The Doctor was about to point out that it could hardly have been guarded against, when the President (who was a better courtier) anticipated him.

"We did not foresee that your Highness, in your Highness' wisdom, would issue this decree," he said humbly.

"True," said Duke Deodonato, who was a just man.

"Would your Highness vouchsafe any explanation—"

"What are the Judges for?" asked Duke Deodonato. "There is the law—let them interpret it."

Whereupon the Judges held that a "man" was not a "woman," and that although every man must marry, no woman need.

"It will make no difference," said the President.

"None at all," said Dr. Fusbius.

Nor, perhaps, would it, seeing that women are ever kind and in no way by nature averse from marriage, had it not become known that Duke Deodonato himself intended to choose a wife from the ladies of his own dominions, and to choose her (according to the advice of Dr. Fusbius, who, in truth, saw little whither his counsel would in the end carry the Duke) without regard to such adventitious matters as rank or wealth, and purely for her beauty, talent, and virtue.

Which resolve being proclaimed, straightway all the ladies of the Duchy, of whatsoever station, calling, age, appearance, wit, or character, conceiving each of them that she, and no other, should become the Duchess, sturdily refused all offers of marriage (although they were many of them as desperately enamored as virtuous ladies may be), and did nought else than walk, drive, ride, and display their charms in the park before the windows of the ducal palace. And thus it fell out that when a week had gone by, no man had obeyed Duke Deodonato's decree, and they were, from sheer want of brides, like to fall into contempt of the law and under the high displeasure of the Duke.

Upon this the President and Dr. Fusbius sought audience of his Highness and humbly laid before him the unforeseen obstacle which had occurred.

"Woman is ever ambitious," said Dr. Fusbius.

"Nay," corrected the President, "they have seen his Highness' person as his Highness has ridden through the city."

Duke Deodonato threw down his pen.

"This is very tiresome," said he, knitting his brows. "My lord, I would be further advised on this matter. Return at the same hour to-morrow."

The next day, Duke Deodonato's forehead had regained its customary smoothness, and his manner was tranquil and assured.

"Our pleasure is," said he to the President, "that, albeit no woman shall be compelled to marry if so be that she be not invited thereunto; yet, if bidden, she shall in no wise refuse, but straightway espouse that man who first after the date of these presents shall solicit her hand."

The President bowed in admiration.

"It is, if I may humbly say so, a practical and wise solution, sir," he said.

"I apprehend that it will remedy the mischief," said Duke Deodonato, not ill pleased.

And doubtless it would have had an effect as altogether satisfactory, excellent, beneficial, salutary, and universal as the wisdom of Duke Deodonato had anticipated from it, had it not fallen out that, on the promulgation of the decree, all the aforesaid ladies of the Duchy, of whatsoever station, calling, age, appearance, wit, or character, straightway, and so swiftly that no man had time wherein to pay his court to them, fled to and shut and bottled and barricaded themselves in houses, castles, cupboards, cellars, stables, lofts, churches, chapels, chests, and every other kind of receptacle whatsoever, and there remained beyond reach of any man, be he whom he would, lest haply one, coming, should ask their hand in marriage, and thus they should lose all prospect of wedding the Duke.

When Duke Deodonato was apprised of this lamentable action on the part of the ladies of the Duchy, he frowned and laid down his pen.

"This is very annoying," said he. "There appears to be a disposition to thwart Our endeavors for the public good."

"It is gross contumacy," said Dr. Fusbius.

"Yet," remarked the President, "inspired by a natural, if ill- disciplined, admiration for his Highness' person."

"The decree is now a fortnight old," observed Duke Deodonato. "Leave me. I will consider further of this matter."

Now even as his Highness spoke a mighty uproar arose under the palace windows, and Duke Deodonato, looking out of the window (which, be it remembered, but for the guidance of Heaven he might not have done), beheld a maiden of wonderful charms struggling in the clutches of two halberdiers of the guard, who were haling her off to prison.

"Bring hither that damsel," said Deodonato.

Presently the damsel, still held by the soldiers, entered the room. Her robe was disheveled and rent, her golden hair hung loose on her shoulders, and her eyes were full of tears.

"At whose suit is she arrested?" asked Deodonato.

"At the suit of the most learned Dr. Fusbius, may it please your Highness."

"Sir," said Dr. Fusbius, "it is true. This lady, grossly contemning your Highness' decree, has refused my hand in marriage."

"Is it true, damsel?" asked Duke Deodonato.

"Hear me, your Highness!" answered she. "I left my dwelling but an instant, for we were in sore straits for—"

"Bread?" asked Deodonato, a touch of sympathy in his voice.

"May it please your Highness, no—pins wherewith to fasten our hair. And, as I ran to the merchant's, this aged man—"

"I am but turned of fifty," interrupted Fusbius.

"And have not yet learned silence!" asked Deodonato severely. "Damsel, proceed!"

"Caught me by my gown as I ran, and—"

"I proposed marriage to her," said Fusbius.

"Nay, if you proposed marriage," she shall marry you," said Deodonato. "By the crown of my fathers, she shall marry you! But what said he, damsel?"

"May it please your Highness, he said that I had the prettiest face in all the Duchy, and that he would have no wife but me; and thereupon he kissed me; and I would have none of him, and I struck him and escaped."

"Send for the Judges," said Duke Deodonato. "And meanwhile keep this damsel and let no man propose marriage to her until Our pleasure be known."

Now, when the Judges were come, and the maiden was brought in and set over against them on the right hand, and the learned Doctor took his stand on the left, Deodonato prayed the Judges that they would perpend carefully and anxiously of the question—using all lore, research, wisdom, discretion, and justice—whether Dr. Fusbius had proposed marriage unto the maiden or no.

"Thus shall Our mind be informed, and we shall deal profitably with this matter," concluded Duke Deodonato.

Upon which arose great debate. For there was one part of the learned men which leaned upon the letter and found no invitation to marriage in the words of Dr. Fusbius; while another part would have it that in all things the spirit and mind of the utterer must be regarded, and that it sorted not with the years, virtues, learning, and position of the said most learned Doctor to suppose that he had spoken such words and sealed the same with a kiss, save under the firm impression, thought, and conviction that he was offering his hand in marriage; which said impression, thought, and conviction were fully and reasonably declared and evident in his actions, manner, bearing, air, and conduct.

"This is very perplexing," said Duke Deodonato, and he knit his brows; for as he gazed upon the beauty of the damsel, it seemed to him a thing unnatural, undesirable, unpalatable, unpleasant, and unendurable, that she should wed Dr. Fusbius.

Yet if such were the law—Duke Deodonato sighed, and he glanced at the damsel: and it chanced that the damsel glanced at Duke Deodonato, and, seeing that he was a proper man and comely, and that his eye spoke his admiration of her, she blushed; and her cheek that had gone white when those of the judges who favored the learned Doctor were speaking, went red as a rose again, and she strove to order her hair, and to conceal the rent that was in her robe. And Duke Deodonato sighed again.

"My lord," he said to the President, "we have heard these wise and erudite men; and, for as much as the matter is difficult, they are divided among themselves, and the staff whereon we leaned is broken. Speak, therefore, your mind."

Then the President of the Council looked earnestly at Duke Deodonato, but the Duke veiled his face with his hand.

"Answer truly," said he, "without fear or favor. So shall you fulfill Our pleasure."

And the President, looking round upon the company, said:

"It is, your Highness, by all reasonable, honest, just, proper, and honorable intendment, as good, sound, full, and explicit an offer of marriage as hath ever been had in this duchy."

"So be it," said Duke Deodonato; and Dr. Fusbius smiled in triumph, while the maiden grew pale again.

"And," pursued the President, "it binds, controls, and rules every man, woman, and child in these your Highness' dominions, and hath the force of law over all."

"So be it," said Deodonato again.

"Saving," added the President, "your Highness only."

There was a movement among the company.

"For," pursued the President, "by the ancient laws, customs, manners, and observances of the Duchy, no decree or law shall in any way whatsoever impair, alter, lessen, or derogate from the high rights, powers, and prerogatives of your Highness, whom may Heaven long preserve. Although, therefore, it be, by and pursuant to your Highness' decree, the sure right of every man in this Duchy to be accepted in marriage of any damsel whom he shall invite thereunto, yet is this right in all respects subject to and controlled by the natural, legal, inalienable, unalterable, and sovereign prerogative of your Highness to marry what damsel soever it shall be your pleasure to bid share your throne. Hence I, in obedience to your Highness' commands, pronounce and declare that this damsel is lawfully and irrevocably bound and affianced to the learned Dr. Fusbius, unless and until it shall please your Highness yourself to demand her hand in marriage. May what I have spoken please your Highness!" And the President sat down.

Duke Deodonato sat a while in thought, and there was silence in the hall. Then he spoke:

"Let all withdraw, saving the damsel only."

And they one and all withdrew, and Duke Deodonato was left alone with the damsel.

Then he arose and gazed long on the damsel; but the damsel would not look on Duke Deodonato.

"How are you called, lady?" asked Duke Deodonato.

"I am called Dulcissima," said she.

"Well named!" said Deodonato softly, and he went to the damsel, and he laid his hand, full gently, on her robe, and he said:

"Dulcissima, you have the prettiest face in all the Duchy, and I will have no wife but you;" and Duke Deodonato kissed the damsel.

The damsel forbore to strike Duke Deodonato, as she had struck Dr. Fusbius. Again her cheek went red, and again pale, and she said:

"I wed no man on compulsion."

"Madam, I am your Sovereign," said Duke Deodonato; and his eyes were on the damsel.

"If you were an Archangel—" cried the damsel.

"Our house is not wont to be scorned of ladies," said Deodonato. "Am I crooked, or baseborn, or a fool?"

"This day in your Duchy women are slaves, and men their masters by your will," said she.

"It is the order of nature," said Deodonato.

"It is not my pleasure," said the damsel.

Then Deodonato laid his hand on his silver bell, for he was very angry.

"Fusbius waits without," said he.

"I will wed him and kill him," cried Dulcissima.

Deodonato gazed on her.

"You had no chance of using the pins," said he, "and the rent in your gown is very sore."

And upon this the eyes of the damsel lost their fire and sought the floor; and she plucked at her girdle, and would not look on Deodonato. And they said outside:

"It is very still in the Hall of the Duke."

Then said Deodonato:

"Dulcissima, what would you?"

"That you repeal your decrees," said she.

Deodonato's brow grew dark; he did not love to go back.

"What I have decreed, I have decreed," said he.

"And what I have resolved, I have resolved," said she.

Deodonato drew near to her.

"And if I repeal the decrees?" said he.

"You will do well," said she.

"And you will wed—"

"Whom I will," said she.

Deodonato turned to the window, and for a space he looked out; and the damsel smoothed her hair and drew her robe, where it was whole, across the rent; and she looked on Deodonato as he stood, and her bosom rose and fell. And she prayed a prayer that no man heard, or, if he heard, might be so base as to tell. But she saw the dark locks of Deodonato's hair and his form, straight as an arrow and tall as a six-foot wand, in the window. And again, outside, they said:

"It is strangely still in the Hall of the Duke."

Then Deodonato turned, and he pressed with his hand on the silver bell, and straightway the Hall was filled with the Councilors, the Judges, and the halberdiers, attentive to hear the will of Deodonato and the fate of the damsel. And the small eyes of Fusbius glowed, and the calm eyes of the President smiled.

"My Cousins, Gentlemen, and my faithful Guard," said Deodonato, "Time, which is Heaven's mighty Instrument, brings counsel. Say! what the Duke has done, shall any man undo?"

Then cried they all, save one:

"No man!"

And the President said:

"Saving the Duke."

"The decrees which I made," said Deodonato, "I unmake. Henceforth let men and maidens in my Duchy marry or not marry as they will, and God give them joy of it."

And all, save Fusbius, cried "Amen!" But Fusbius cried:

"Your Highness, it is demonstrated beyond cavil; ay, to the satisfaction of your Highness—"

"This is very tedious," said Deodonato. "Let him speak no more!"

And again he drew near to Dulcissima, and there, before them all, he fell on his knee. And a murmur ran through the hall.

"Madam," said Deodonato, "if you love me, wed me. And, if you love me not, depart in peace and in honor; and I, Deodonato, will live my life alone."

Then the damsel trembled, and barely did Deodonato catch her words:

"There are many men here," said she.

"It is not given to Princes," said Deodonato, "to be alone. Nevertheless, if you will, leave me alone." And the damsel bent low, so that the breath of her mouth stirred the hair on Deodonato's head, and he shivered as he knelt.

"My Prince and my King!" said she.

And Deodonato shot to his feet, and before them all he kissed her, and, turning, spoke:

"As I have wooed, let every man in this Duchy woo. As I have won, let every man that is worthy win. For, unless he so woo, and unless he so win, vain is his wooing, and vain is his winning, and a fig for his wedding, say I, Deodonato! I, that was Deodonato, and now am—Deodonato and Dulcissima."

And a great cheer rang out in the Hall, and Fusbius fled to the door; and they tore his gown as he went and cursed him for a knave. But the President raised his voice aloud and cried:

"May Heaven preserve your Highnesses—and here's a blessing on all windows!"

And that is the reason why you will find (if you travel there, as I trust you may, for nowhere are the ladies fairer or the men so gallant) more windows in the Duchy of Deodonato than anywhere in the wide world besides. For the more windows, the wider the view; and the wider the view, the more pretty damsels do you see; and the more pretty damsels you see, the more jocund a thing is life—and that is what the men of the Duchy love—and not least, Duke Deodonato, whom, with his bride Dulcissima, may Heaven long preserve!

Chapter 8

All's Well That Ends Well

There was once—the date is of no moment—a Sultan, and he had a Vizier named Ashimullah. This minister was a wise man, much trusted by his master; but he was held in some suspicion and dislike at the court because he had been born—or, if that be doubtful, had at least been bred—a Christian, and had been originally a prisoner of the Sultan's armies.

But Ashimullah, for reasons which intimately concerned his own head, but need not concern anybody else's, promptly found the true path; and, having professed a ready conversion to the tenets of Islam, rose rapidly to a high place in the service of the Sultan, so that his promotion never ceased until he was installed in the office of Grand Vizier. Yet, remembering his discreditable past, the Sultan was accustomed to exact from him the fullest and most minute observance of his religious duties. To such observance Ashimullah submitted, comforting himself with the example of Naaman the Syrian; for Ashimullah was still, in secret, a Christian, and his adherence to Islam was only a polite concession to public feeling. But there was one point on which his conscience struck him sorely, and this was no other than the question of wives. Ashimullah had one wife, a lady of great beauty and remarkable accomplishments, and for the life of him he could not see how, consistently with the religion which he held in his heart and with the honor that he owed to the lady, he could take any other wife. Such an act appeared to him to be a deadly sin, for it was most plainly held and laid down by the rules of his religion, and had moreover been amply proved by experience, that one wife was enough for any man. Therefore when the Sultan, hearing that Ashimullah had but one wife, and considering the thing very suspicious and unnatural, sent for him, and required him to order his establishment on a scale more befitting his present exalted position, Ashimullah was in sad perplexity. To obey was to sin, to refuse was likely to cost him his life; for if his master suspected the sincerity of his conversion, his shrift would be short. In this quandary Ashimullah sought about for excuses.

"O Commander of the Faithful, I am a poor man, and wives are sources of expense," said Ashimullah.

"My treasury is open to the most faithful of my servants," said the Sultan.

"A multitude of women in a house breeds strife," urged Ashimullah.

"He who governs an empire should be able to govern his own house," remarked the Sultan.

"I have no pleasure in the society of women," pleaded Ashimullah.

"It is not a question of pleasure," said the Sultan solemnly, and Ashimullah thought that he saw signs of suspicion on his master's august face. Therefore he prostrated himself, crying that he submitted to the imperial will, and would straightway take another wife.

"I do not love a grudging obedience," said the Sultan.

"I will take two!" cried Ashimullah.

"Take three," said the Sultan; and with this he dismissed Ashimullah, giving him the space of a week in which to fulfill the command laid upon him.

"Surely I am a most unhappy man," mused Ashimullah. "For if I do not obey, I shall be put to death; and if I do obey, I fear greatly that I shall be damned." And he went home looking so sorrowful and perplexed that all men conceived that he was out of favor with the Sultan.

Now Ashimullah, being come to his house, went immediately to his wife, and told her of the Sultan's commands, adding that the matter was a sore grief to him, and not less on her account than on his own. "For you know well, Star of my Heart," said he, "that I desire no wife but you!"

"I know it well, Ashimullah," answered Lallakalla tenderly.

"Moreover, I fear that I shall be damned," whispered Ashimullah.

"I'm sure you would," said Lallakalla.

Three days later it was reported through all the city, on the authority of Hassan, the chief and confidential servant of the Vizier, that Ashimullah, having procured three slaves of great beauty at an immense cost, had wedded them all, and thus completed the number of wives allowed to him by the Law of the Prophet. The first was rosy-cheeked with golden hair; the second's complexion was olive, and her locks black as night; the third had a wonderful pallor, and tresses like burnished gold.

"Thus," added Hassan, "since my lady Lallakalla's hair is brown, his Highness the Vizier enjoys, as is his most just due, all varieties of beauty."

When these things came to the ears of the Sultan, he was greatly pleased with the prompt obedience of Ashimullah, and sent him a large sum of money and his own miniature, magnificently set in diamonds. Moreover, he approved highly of the taste that Ashimullah had displayed in his choice, and regretted very deeply that he could not behold the charms of the wives of the Vizier. Nay, so great was his anxiety concerning them that he determined to send one of his Sultanas to pay a visit to the harem of Ashimullah, in order that, while seeming to render honor to Ashimullah, she might report to him of the beauty of Ashimullah's wives.

"We must make ready for the visit of the Sultana," observed Lallakalla, with a smile.

When the Sultana returned from her visit, the Sultan came to her without delay, and she said:

"O Most Translucent Majesty, wonderful indeed are the wives of Ashimullah! For as they came before me, one after another, I did not know which of them to call most beautiful; for the brown hair, the golden, the black, and the ruddy are all most fair to see. I would that your Majesty could behold them!"

"I would that I could!" said the Sultan, stroking his beard.

"Yet, O Sultan, since all men are mortal, and it is not given to any to be perfectly happy in this world, know that there is an alloy in the happiness of Ashimullah the Vizier. For these most lovely ladies have, each and all of them, so strong and vehement a temper and so great a reciprocal hatred, that Ashimullah is compelled to keep them apart, each in her own chamber, and by no means can they be allowed to come together for an instant. Not even my presence would have restrained them, and therefore I saw each alone."

"I do not object to a little temper," observed the Sultan, stroking his beard again. "It is a sauce to beauty, and keeps a man alive."

"It is only toward one another that they are fierce," said the Sultana. "For all spoke with the greatest love of Ashimullah, and with the most dutiful respect."

"I do not see on what account they are so fond of Ashimullah," said the Sultan, frowning.

That night the Sultan did not once close his eyes, for he could think of nothing save the marvelous and varied beauty of the wives of the Vizier; and between the rival charms of the black, the brown, the ruddy, and the golden, his Majesty was so torn and tossed about that, when he rose, his brow was troubled and his cheek pale. And being no longer able to endure the torment that he suffered, he sent the Sultana again to visit the house of Ashimullah, bidding her observe most carefully which of the ladies was in truth most beautiful. But the Sultana, having returned, professed herself entirely unable to set any one of Ashimullah's wives above any other in any point of beauty. "For they are all," said she, "and each in her own way, houris for beauty."

"And this man was a Christian dog once!" murmured the Sultan. Then his brow suddenly grew smooth, and he observed:

"Ashimullah himself will know; and, indeed, it is time that I gave a new sign of my favor to my trusted servant Ashimullah."

Therefore he sent for Ashimullah, and spoke to him with unbounded graciousness.

"Ashimullah, my faithful servant," said he, "I am mindful to confer upon you a great and signal favor; desiring to recognize not only your services to my throne, but also and more especially your ready and willing obedience in the matter of your wives. Therefore I have decided to exalt you and your household in the eyes of all the Faithful, and of the whole world, by taking from your house a wife for myself."

When Ashimullah heard this he went very pale, although, in truth, what the Sultan proposed to do was always held the highest of honors.

"And since so good and loyal a servant," pursued the Sultan, "would desire to offer to his Sovereign nothing but the best of all that he has, tell me, O Ashimullah, which of your wives is fairest, that I may take her and exalt her as I have proposed."

Ashimullah was now in great agitation, and he stammered in his confusion:

"My wives are indeed fair; but, O Most Potent and Fearful Majesty, they have, one and all, most diabolical tempers."

"Surely by now I have learned how to deal with the tempers of women," said the Sultan, raising his brows. "Come, Ashimullah; tell me which is fairest."

Then Ashimullah, being at his wits' end, and catching at any straw in order to secure a little delay, declared that it was utterly impossible to say that any one of his wives was fairer than any other, for they were all perfectly beautiful.

"But describe them to me, one by one," commanded the Sultan.

So Ashimullah described his wives one by one to the Sultan, using most exalted eloquence, and employing every simile, metaphor, image, figure, and trope that language contains, in the vain attempt to express adequately the surpassing beauty of those ladies; yet he was most careful to set no one above any other and to distribute the said similes, metaphors, images, figures, and tropes, with absolute impartiality and equality among them.

"By Allah, it is difficult!" said the Sultan, pulling his beard fretfully. "I will consider your several descriptions, and send for you again in a few days, Ashimullah."

So Ashimullah went home and told Lallakalla all that had passed between the Sultan and himself, and how the Sultan proposed to take one of his wives, but could not make up his mind which lady he should prefer.

"But, alas! it is all one to me, whichever he chooses," cried Ashimullah, in despair.

"It is all one to me also," cried Lallakalla. "But, be sure, dear Ashimullah, that the Sultan has some purpose in this delay. Let us wait and see what he does. It may be that we need not yet despair."

But Ashimullah would not be comforted, and cried out that he had done better never to forswear his religion, but to have died at once, as a holy martyr.

"It is too late to think of that," said Lallakalla.

Now, had not the Sultan been most lamentably bewildered and most amazingly dazzled by the conflicting charms of the wives of Ashimullah, beyond doubt he would not have entertained nor carried out a project so impious and irreligious as that which his curiosity and passion now led him into. But being unable to eat or drink or rest until he was at ease on the matter, he determined, all piety and law and decorum to the contrary notwithstanding, to look upon the faces of Ashimullah's wives with his own eyes, and determine for himself to whom the crown of beauty belonged, and whether the brown or the black, or the golden or the ruddy, might most properly and truthfully lay claim to it. But this resolution he ventured to communicate to nobody, save to the faithful and dutiful wife whom he had sent before to visit the house of Ashimullah. She, amazed, tried earnestly to dissuade him, but seeing he was not to be turned, at last agreed to second his designs, and enable him to fulfill his purpose. "Though I fear no good will come of it," she sighed.

"I wonder which is in truth the fairest!" murmured the Sultan. And he sent word to Ashimullah that the Sultana would visit his wives on the evening of that day.

"All will be ready for her," said Lallakalla, when she received the message from her husband.

But in the afternoon the Sultan sent men into the bazaar, and these men caught Hassan, Ashimullah's servant, as he came to make his daily purchases, and carried him to the Sultan, with whom he was closeted for hard on an hour. When he came out Hassan returned home, shaking his head sorrowfully, but patting his purse comfortably; whence it appears that he suffered from a conflict of feelings, his mind being ill at ease, but his purse heavier. And when in the evening the Sultana came, attended only by one tall, formidable, and inky-black attendant, Hassan ushered her into the reception room of the harem, telling her that Lallakalla, the first wife of his master, would attend her immediately. Then he went out, and, having brought in the big black slave very secretly, set him in the antechamber of the room where the Sultana was, and hid him there, behind a high screen. And Hassan pierced a hole in the screen, so that the big slave could see what passed in the antechamber without being seen himself. Then Hassan, still shaking his head, but also patting his purse, went to summon Lallakalla. But the big black slave lay quiet behind the screen.

Presently Lallakalla passed through and entered the room where the Sultana was. A few moments later Ashimullah came in, carrying over one arm several robes of silk and in the other a large box or trunk. Ashimullah looked round cautiously, but saw nobody; the big black slave held his breath, but laid his hand on the scimitar that he wore. Ashimullah waited. Then Lallakalla came out.

"Yes, of a truth this brown-haired one is most lovely," thought the big slave. "It would seem impossible that the others can be so lovely. Moreover, she looks amiable enough. Yet I must see the others. Which will come next?" And he composed himself to wait for the next, not caring whether she were the ruddy, the golden, or the black, so that she came quickly.

But, to the amazement of the slave, Lallakalla tore off the silken robe she wore and cried to her husband, "Give me the blue robe— yes, and the golden hair." And, having put on the blue robe, she took from Ashimullah's hand something that he had taken from the square box, and put it on her head. Then Ashimullah gave her a smaller box, and, taking out paints and brushes and a mirror, she made a complexion for herself. And thus she was transformed into a golden-haired lady with cheeks of rosy red, and in this guise she passed in to the Sultana's presence.

"The dog!" thought the slave. "Then he took only two wives more!"

Presently Lallakalla came forth; and all happened as before, save that she stained her face to an olive tint and put on a wig of coal-black hair.

"By the Prophet!" thought the slave, "he took but one wife more!"

Yet again Lallakalla came out from visiting the Sultana, and on this occasion she hastily donned a robe of red, sprinkled white powder over her cheeks, and set on her head a most magnificent structure of ruddy hair. Thus arrayed she went again into the room where the Sultana was.

"By Allah, the dog took no other wife at all!" thought the slave, and, looking through his spy-hole, he saw Ashimullah making off in great haste, carrying the box and the robes with him. Then Hassan came and led the slave back by the way they had come to the place where he awaited the Sultana.

"This wife of Ashimullah is a wonderful woman," said the Sultan to himself, as he lay awake that night. "Behold, she is in herself a multitude!"

Early the next morning Ashimullah was summoned to the palace, and at once ushered into the presence of the Sultan.

"O Ashimullah, I have reflected," said the Sultan, "and I desire that you will send me that wife of yours who has ruddy hair. For although the choice is difficult, yet I think that she must be the fairest of them all."

Ashimullah, knowing not what to say, prostrated himself and promised obedience; then, having withdrawn from the presence, he ran back home as fast as he could lay his feet to the ground, and sought out Lallakalla. With her he talked for some time; then he returned to the palace, weeping and wringing his hands.

"What ails you, Ashimullah?" asked the Sultan.

"Alas! O Light of the World, a pestilence has fallen on my house, and my wife with the ruddy hair lies dead."

"We must resign ourselves to the will of Heaven," said the Sultan. "Yet I will not recall the favor I had destined for you. Send me the wife that has coal-black hair, Ashimullah."

"Alas! Most Mighty One, misfortunes crowd upon me. That grace-less wife has fled from me in company with a fishmonger," groaned Ashimullah.

"You are well quit of her, and so also am I," remarked the Sultan. "Yet I am not to be turned from my benevolent purpose, and rather than fail in doing you honor, I will accept the wife with the golden hair."

"Alas! and alas! High and Potent Majesty, Heaven has set its wrath upon me. As she rowed this morning, the boat upset, and she, my golden-haired beauty, was drowned!" And Ashimullah laid his head on the ground and sobbed pitifully.

"Of a truth you are afflicted. Yet do not despair, I will comfort you, my good Ashimullah," said the Sultan. "Weep no more. Send me the wife with the brown hair, and all shall be well. By Allah! I am a man that hears reason, and does not exact more than Fate will allow! A man can give only what he has. I shall be well pleased with her of the brown hair, Ashimullah."

Then Ashimullah crawled to the feet of the Sultan, and said:

"Ruler of the World, great is the honor that you purpose for the meanest of your servants. Yet behold, if I send my wife with the brown hair, I shall have no wife at all; for the others are gone, and my house will be altogether desolate."

The Sultan smiled down at Ashimullah. Then he bent and took him by the hands and raised him up. And he spoke to him in a tone of most tender and friendly reproach:

"Indeed, Ashimullah," said he, "you wrong me in your thoughts, supposing that I would leave your house desolate, or that I would receive without bestowing. Such is not the custom of great princes, nor is it my custom. But where we take we give fourfold of what is given to us. Be of good cheer, and grieve no more either for the wives who are dead or for the brown-haired wife whom it is my gracious pleasure to accept from you. For I will send you four wives; and thus you shall be as you were before your misfortunes, and before you gave me your brown-haired wife. And if the color of their hair does not please you (for it seems that you are curious in these matters, O Ashimullah), I think that you have means to set right what is wrong, and to array the head of each in the color that you love best." And, as he said this, the Sultan looked very full and significantly in the face of Ashimullah.

But Ashimullah turned and went out, full of fear; for he perceived that the Sultan had discovered his secret and that he had been betrayed by Hassan his servant, and he feared for his life, because of the trick that he had played upon the Sultan, besides being greatly afflicted to think that now indeed there was no escape, but he must have four wives. Moreover, although this could not stand beside the question of his salvation, he regretted greatly the losing of Lallakalla, whom the Sultan took from him. And as he told Lallakalla all that had passed, he wept; but she bade him be of good cheer, and, having comforted him, withdrew to her apartments, and was very busy there all the afternoon.

In the evening came a litter from the palace, and with it a letter from the Sultan, commanding that Lallakalla should come, and bidding Ashimullah to expect his four wives the next day. Accordingly Ashimullah, having divorced Lallakalla according to the formalities of the law, set her in the litter, and she, being brought to the palace, was soon visited by the Sultan, who was full of curiosity to see her. But, when he entered, he gave a loud cry of surprise. For, behold, the hair on Lallakalla's head was red. But then he smiled and said to her:

"Take off the wig, my daughter."

"I obey," said she, "but I pray you to look away while I obey."

So the Sultan looked away, and, when he turned again, her hair was golden.

"Take that off also," said the Sultan, turning his head away. And when he looked again her hair was coal-black.

"Take that off also," said the Sultan.

"I obey," said Lallakalla, and the Sultan turned away.

"Now," said he, "I will behold your own brown hair," and he turned to her. But again he cried out in surprise and horror. For there was no brown hair on Lallakalla's head, but her head was bare and shaven as clean as the ball of ivory on the staff that the Sultan carried.

"Heaven forbid," said Lallakalla meekly, "that I should come to the Light of the Universe with hair of the color that he hates; for he chose every color sooner than my poor color. Therefore I have left the brown hair for Ashimullah, for he loves it, and I have brought my lord the colors that my lord loves." And with this she laid the three wigs of black hair, of golden, and of ruddy at the Sultan's feet, and stood herself before him with her shaven poll.

Then the Sultan, seeing that Lallakalla looked very ludicrous with her shaven poll, burst out laughing. And he came and took her by the hand, and said to her:

"Behold a woman who loves her husband better than her beauty, and to be his wife rather than mine! Return, then, to Ashimullah and be his wife again."

"My lord," said she, "suffer me also to take back with me the other wives of Ashimullah," and she pointed to the heads of hair that lay upon the ground.

"Take them," said he, laughing. "And since Ashimullah has already four wives and yet will give me no wife, why, neither will I give Ashimullah any wives. But he shall have the four wives that he had before, and all the city shall hear of the beauty and the virtue of Ashimullah's wives."

So Lallakalla went home in great joy, and put on her own hair, which she had fashioned into a wig, and went in to Ashimullah. And they dwelt happily together, there being no differences in their household, save in the color of Lallakalla's hair from day to day. But the Sultan raised a pillar of many-colored marble, black and gold, brown and red, and inscribed it, "To the Virtues of the Wives of Ashimullah the Vizier." And henceforward none troubled Ashimullah concerning his wives.

Hassan, however, was most justly put to death.

www.ingramcontent.com/pod-product-compliance
Lightning Source LLC
Chambersburg PA
CBHW022044170626
46808CB00003B/1356